THE SAFE ROOM

DAVID LOPERA

Published by

Shock & Suspense

www.davidloperafiction.com

Cover art by Sandeep Karunakaran (Sanskarans).

www.instagram.com / sanskaransart

www.artstation.com / sanskarans

www.facebook.com / Sanskarans

To my mother, Nena,
and my father, Pacho (1938-2022).

"The prince of darkness is a gentleman!"
— William Shakespeare, *King Lear*

*"Every act of rebellion expresses a nostalgia for innocence
and an appeal to the essence of being."*
— Albert Camus, *The Rebel*

Warning: This book contains graphic content. Reader discretion is advised.

PART ONE

JUNE 30

Dear Diary,

Today is my first day at Palisades Girls Academy. My parents dropped me off here this morning, and oh my god, it sucks *soo* bad. Let me begin by telling you about my idiot roommate. She thinks that just because we're roommates and I'm forced to bunk with her, that all of a sudden we're gonna be best friends. Well, she's wrong. Wrong, wrong, wrong! I hate her already.

Shortly after getting here, I had to meet with a psychologist (for intake), and when I got back to the room, she had gone through my things! I still can't believe it. She fucking asked if she could borrow one of my tops. *Who* would do that? Apparently my psycho roommate would. She also doesn't ever stop talking. I've known her for like half a day and I already know her goddamn life story. I'll refer to her as Chatterbox from here on out. I signed a confidentiality waiver, and we're not really supposed to talk (or write) about what goes on here or mention people's names. Blah, blah, blah. I'll respect that. But, they can't tell me I can't write in my diary. That's my personal business. Maybe one day I'll tell you their *real* names.

Anyway, today was a really long day and I'm really tired. I had to wake up at the butt crack of dawn to drive up to this forsaken place with my parents. It was a five and change hour drive. We took the interstate most of the way, then got on some twisty roads that eventually spit us out all the way up here in the sticks. Once I'd arrived, I had to go through the whole intake process, which took *over* two hours. It was an endless heap of papers my parents had to sign. The screws even made me sign a few forms. Oh, when I write about or mention screws, I'm referring to the brutes in charge here. I may also refer to them as pigs or sarge if I'm feeling kind. I had to meet all the head screws, then I had that stupid meeting with the psychologist. There's a lot more that happened, but I don't have it in me tonight to tell you everything. I'd be here all night and my tank's been emptied. The lights have to go off at nine and it's already past that. I'm currently writing underneath my blanket and I'm using a portable nightlight I brought, but I don't want to get in trouble. It was one of the few personal items they allowed me to keep with me. They were very selective as to what clothes I was allowed to bring in. Nothing too scanty, which isn't an issue with me since I'm what people would call a "tomboy". Anyway, if someone were to peer through the window into our room, they'd see something that might resemble the shape of a ghost glowing faintly underneath a blanket. I can't risk them taking my journal. It's my escape. Time to turn off my light so no one sees me. I'll be back tomorrow. Peace.

JULY 1

Dear Diary,

Today was a *reeeeally* long day. I almost didn't pick up my journal, but I forced myself to write down some of the key things that happened. I *have* to tell you about this place.

But before I do, I should probably start by telling you about how I ended up here. I'm not a bad girl in the usual sense. Trust me, I've already met some really troubled girls here and I've known some real pieces of work on the outside, so I'm nothing in comparison to those gals. Take Chatterbox, for example—she's in here because she's just plain crazy. Apparently the whole world is against her. Her parents, her friends, her family, her school, her doctors, the bus driver, the mailman, you name it… everyone has it out for her. At least according to her, they do.

What I've gathered from what she's told me, though, is that she has a really bad pill problem. She's on like ten different medications (possibly more?). Antipsychotics and painkillers. She's only told me a few stories about her pill-popping escapades, and I'm not sure how she's still alive.

There's another girl I met that's also batshit crazy, but I'll tell you about her a little later.

Let me get back to the reason I'm here.

It all started freshman year of high school. I've always gotten along pretty well with the boys. Patrick, one of my best friends, often says I'm like *one of the guys*. I've always been close with Patrick and Doug. Doug is cool too, but I get the feeling he wants to be more than just friends. Nothing's happened between us ever, though. I don't really like him in *that* way. I really like him as a person, as a human.

So, back to freshman year.

We all grew up together on the same street and we ended up going to the same Catholic school—St. Mary's Prep. Our parents had arrived at the same conclusion that it would be better to fork up the cash and send us to private school (that it was a parochial school was an afterthought) instead of chancing it at the local public school, which is a warzone amongst hormonal savages. Even though that's where I ultimately ended up, it wasn't the ideal school for any of us. The public schools in our town are rough.

Patrick, Doug, and I tried to make the best of it at St. Mary's Prep. I should probably mention Doug, who's a covert overachiever, still goes there. My dad would call him an *academic* and a *paragon*. Guess it just comes naturally for some than for others.

I, on the other hand, didn't make it past my second month of my freshman year at St. Mary's. I couldn't even hack it past the first marking period.

There was a stuck up girl that really had it out for me. Her name was Jen and she came from a wealthy family. Her father was a doctor. Big frickin' whoop. What really got under my skin was she'd talk to you like you were literal dirt—as if she was Marie fucking Antoinette. She would even address teachers condescendingly. But rarely was she ever reprimanded. Her father was a big donor to the school. Anyway, I somehow caught her attention, most likely because I was different from her little prissy girlfriends. She thought she was cute by calling me names. I let it slide the first few times she talked smack. The first time was in biology. Then it happened in the lunchroom. Then it happened after school on the way to the bus. It got to the point where I couldn't let her say those mean, nasty things to me, so… I let her have it.

We were in phys ed class and she called me a dyke. My response was a quick jab to her mouth. I used to like watching old MMA fights and I'm actually a really big boxing fan. Canelo Álvarez is my absolute favorite. When my fist landed, the girl's head jerked back, and in a few seconds, there was blood gushing everywhere, saturating the girl's PE uniform. She never saw it coming. Most of the others were really freaked out. I remember seeing some students hovering around with their mouths agape, looking absolutely horrified. A few students were elated by what I did and cheered me on. It was all smiles and flattery in front of her, but behind her back they'd vilify.

Back to the punch. It landed so perfectly. It felt sort of surreal to hurt someone like that, with such force. I'd seen it in boxing matches and in movies, but in real life, it was like I was in a dream and everyone else there was also a part of it too.

To my misfortune, it wasn't a dream. I'd gotten expelled immediately and got transferred to the public school after that little incident. Things there didn't go all that well, either. It's sort of a long story, but in a nutshell, I got into more fights. The girls at the public school actually put up a challenge. I got knocked around quite a bit there. I think I suffered a concussion during one tussle. I was hit so hard in the nose, I remember seeing a flash of white and then the world went black. My friends who witnessed it said my legs collapsed under me and I was sprawled out on the floor for a solid five minutes. They told me they were afraid that maybe I'd been killed. After that, I understood firsthand what it means for your lights to be turned off. It took a lot longer to get expelled at the public school, but that's eventually what happened.

After my expulsion, my parents tried homeschooling me. They started by hiring a tutoring agency. It was one tutor after another for a while. I wasn't making adequate progress and flunked nearly all of my classes, along with all of those dreaded state exams. Guess school just isn't for me. It might not be for everybody, ya know? My parents really tried for a while. I've got to really give it to them. They spent a small fortune attempting to help me turn my life around, but maybe I just need to accept the fact that I'm a bad egg. They needed to accept that fact too, I guess. It must be a hard fact of life for them to stomach when you're their *little angel* (that's what my dad used to call me up until I was about seven or eight), but really, they have a loose cannon on their hands. A loose cannon that school administrators have dubbed a *terror*. During a meeting with Ms. Babcock (the principal at St. Mary's), she told my parents I wasn't merely a disciplinary case. I was a social contagion. I felt a pang of remorse and shame when I heard that one.

So that about sums up how I ended up here at Palisades. That's my story and I'm sticking to it. But, the point of telling you all that is I still think I'm not nearly as crazy as some of these freaks. I mean, some of these girls I've met in just two days are flat out bonkers.

Let me tell you about the girl who's batshit crazy. I'll refer to her as Batgirl. Pun intended.

Today, after lunch, we met with the counselors and had our first counseling session. As it turns out, we're forced to attend counseling five times a week. Yes, you heard me correctly. *Five* times! I'm not kidding. To make matters worse, it's in a group setting. They've split us up into small groups of four. Oh my effing God. It's so awful. It's the worst thing in the world. I wish they would just let me hang out in my room and stare at the walls instead.

My group consists of yours truly, my roommate Chatter-box, Batgirl, and a quiet girl who makes me kind of nervous because at first glance she *seems* normal, but then it makes me wonder what she did to be put in here amongst the crazies. I'll refer to her as Helen Keller.

We met our counselors—Jack and Jill. I wish I was kidding. Those are their names, like for real. They were high-energy and extremely exhausting people to be around. Not to mention they're extra pretentious, especially Jill. She's long-winded and rambles on and on and on. It's easy to check out so who the hell knows what she was talking about.

They sat us in a small circle and the fuckers made us tell

each other one thing that we like, and one thing that makes us tick. You really get to know someone during this activity.

Batgirl shared first.

"One thing that makes me tick is…" she twirled her hair like a small child as she spoke. "Humidity."

"Why does humidity make you tick?" Jack asked with a wide smile.

"Because it fucks up my hair. Every time I get it just how I want it, it poofs." She threw out her hands from her head, showing us what her hair does under such calamitous circumstances. "It's so goddamn annoying!" she cried. "Every fucking time."

"All right, all right. We need to refrain from using profanities when we're here. As a matter of fact, we shouldn't cuss at all while at Palisades," Jill said, shaking her head. "If you curse again, you'll be removed from the group and you'll be sent to the Safe Room."

I perked up when I heard that term. The *Safe Room*. What the hell is that?

"You all signed the contract," Jack reminded us. "In case you didn't read it, or you forgot what it stated, you all agreed that you wouldn't use any curse words while in recovery."

"Ugh…fuck. But I *like* to curse," Batgirl groaned.

Jill sighed. "Let's work on not cursing, please." She glowered at Batgirl. "Starting now."

Batgirl lowered her head, then muttered, "Sure thing."

"So, what's one thing that you like?" Jack asked, with the fakest enthusiasm I've ever witnessed.

Mmmmmmm. Batgirl thought for a moment. "I like dick, that's for sure." She let out a crazy laugh.

Everyone just stared at her wondering if they'd heard her correctly.

"Honey…" Jill began. "You need to work on not being so profane. If you do it again, you'll be placed in time-out." Jill wasn't smiling anymore. She continued, her tone unforgiving. "That's your last and final warning. Now, I'd like you to share out with the group, but we can't have you speaking that way in front of the other girls," Jill's eyes moved, settling on Jack. "Or, staff for that matter." Jill placed her hands on her lap and looked at Batgirl in a serious sort of way. "How about you try and share what you enjoy using more appropriate language? Using more refined language."

"OK..." Batgirl said. "I like boys. I like doing stuff with them."

"Now, that's much better," Jill said. She was smiling again. Her teeth were perfect and white like a model in a toothpaste commercial. "Let's all try to keep what we share at the PG level." She panned around, looking at each one of us, with her fake, glued-on smile.

Jill settled her gaze on me. "Would you like to share, Sue?"

"What would you like me to share?"

"Someone wasn't paying attention when they should've been," the cunt said snidely, as if she were admonishing a five-year old. She went on: "You can share something you like or something you enjoy doing. You could also share something you don't enjoy. But we'd like you to share something."

I rolled my eyes. *This activity is so lame,* I thought. "I like going to the mall," I said, unenthusiastically.

"That's great!" Jill said, clapping her hands together. "What do you like doing at the mall?"

Kill me. Kill me now. Maybe my parents should have just sent me to jail, instead.

"Uh, shopping, going to the food court, checking out the boys, hanging with my boys." It was impossible to hide the boredom from my voice. "You know, regular things girls my age do when they go to the mall."

"That's great, Sue," Jill said. She was clearly annoyed with me, but she couldn't knock my response since I hadn't cursed and I'd played along with her stupid game.

Jill's gaze moved on to Helen Keller. "Helen," Jill said, way too excited. "Your turn."

Helen stared at the floor. She gripped the side of her chair with both hands and swung her legs back and forth, coyly, the way a small child would. She wore athletic arm bands around her wrists. I wondered if she played softball or basketball and just got used to wearing them all the time.

"I…" Helen began. "I…"

Everyone's eyes were on Helen. *Let it out, girl.*

"I hear voices in my head," she whispered.

Batgirl broke out laughing. "Fucking hell," she shrieked.

Oh, Christ. That explains it, then.

Jack and Jill both looked at each other and frowned.

"What do the voices say?" Jack asked.

"Sometimes…" Helen gazed up at Jack. Her eyes were swirling with madness. "They tell me to get a hold of something sharp and start cutting."

"Okay," Jill said, then stood up and clapped her hands together. She seemed to clap often after saying something that seemed important. "That'll be it for today. Thank you all for sharing. We know it's not always easy, but it allows us to get to know each other better. We're going to continue this tomorrow. Today was a great start."

"Yes. Today was a great start," Jack said, almost robotically.

We were escorted out of the room and led back to the common area where we congregated with the rest of the girls. As we were ushered out, Jill asked Helen to hang back and they must've taken her somewhere else because I didn't see her the rest of the day. Maybe they'd stuck her in a padded room and strapped her in a straightjacket. *I hear voices in my head.* What in the actual fuck?

After that, we had dinner and I really hate to be the bearer of bad news, but there's nothing special about the food at this place. It sucks. I'm sure my parents are spending a pretty penny keeping me here, and they could definitely do better with their cuisine, but that's a story for another day. There are many more pressing matters that need to be addressed first.

All right. I'm signing off now. I can't wait to find out what exciting adventures await me at Palisades tomorrow (Not!). If it gets any worse, maybe I'll start hearing voices in my fucking head and I'll look for something sharp and I'll start cutting. I'm going to try to call my parents tomorrow and beg them to let me come home. Jill told me I can phone home tomorrow. Anyway, I'm going to stop writing now. I need to hide my journal underneath my mattress because I don't trust anyone here, and I really don't want anyone reading what I think about them. Until tomorrow. Peace out.

JULY 2

Dear Diary,

Today was a really busy day. We were woken up at 6 a.m., as usual, and had breakfast.

I'm trying to avoid Chatterbox. She seeks me out, wanting to sit near me during all the meals, but she's extremely annoying. I'm finding it very difficult holding back from punching her in her mouth. Maybe that would put a lid on her loquaciousness.

Last night, she tried talking my ear off after it was lights out. I told her to quit her yapping or I'd climb up there (Chatterbox has the top bunk, I have the bottom) and beat her to oblivion. I don't think I've ever met anyone as annoying as her. Hopefully she gets the idea, or else I might thump her. I'm trying to be good, though. Maybe if I behave, I can somehow convince my parents to let me go back home. I really miss Pat and Doug. I want to tell them about this awful place so bad, but I'm not even sure when the next time I'll talk to them will be. I can't exactly call whomever I want. Actually, the more I think about it, this place is just like a prison. Eek!

Back to breakfast. Just as I sat down to chow on the slop I was served, some big girl started to tweak. She stood up at her table and screamed at the top of her lungs, "These eggs are fucking disgusting! *Who* could eat this shit?!" She leapt up on top of the cafeteria table, looking like an enraged chimp, then flung her food tray. Her throw had some real teeth to it and hit a girl point blank in the back of the head who was sitting five feet away. The eggs slopped down the backside of her head, and the bread slapped off her back. Then the big girl yelled, "How are you people able to sleep at night? With the garbage you serve us!"

The gal was furious with the mush they were serving us,

and rightly so. I was pretty upset about it myself, but I decided that I just wouldn't eat that much. I was trying to watch my figure, anyway. Maybe a little dieting would help me tighten up some fat around my midsection.

The hefty girl, though, was wilding out, and it didn't seem like she was going to stop either. Two large goons who looked like security (it was the first time I'd seen them) ran in and restrained her. A female nurse, trailing behind, quickly made her way over and shot her with a sedative. It only took a few seconds for the big girl to wilt over in the men's grasp. They strained to lug her out of the cafeteria, all docile and narcotized, as everyone watched in silence. There was a woman watching from the cafeteria doors who stood out. It was the first time I'd seen her but she seemed important. She stood ramrod straight, her hair a golden, lustrous mane. *Who was she?* She *must* be important, judging by her crisp linen blazer and pantsuit. Jack hovered just behind her, looking like a willing pawn placed exactly where she required him.

I glanced around and some of the other girls' eyes were filled with fear. *Where were they taking her?*

I suddenly thought of Helen. I scanned the cafeteria, searching for her, realizing that I hadn't seen her since therapy the day before. She was nowhere to be seen.

Turning toward the short girl next to me, I asked, "Where do you think they're taking her?"

"To the Safe Room," she answered.

"What's the Safe Room?"

"It's where they take all the girls who misbehave."

I felt a chill spread up my back.

"Have you been there?" I asked.

"No. Never been," she said tightly. "And I'm going to make sure it stays that way."

Safe Room. The name seemed to drain the light from the room. I had a hunch that whatever went on there, was far from safe. *Where* was the Safe Room?

~

Later that morning, we had our counseling session, but besides Helen not being there (she was still MIA), it was pretty uneventful. I won't go into much detail since not much happened. Jill, wearing her synthetic smile, which had turned into a frightening rictus, berated us with more uncomfortable questions. Jack, her creepy lackey, agreed with everything she said, nodding like a devout cult member. I noticed he seemed to be staring at Batgirl sort of strangely. *No, not staring*, I thought. *More like ogling*. Real sus. She was quite attractive, if I'm being honest. Bastard better not be getting any ideas. If he tried anything on her, or on any of the girls (including me), I'd punch his lights out. I'll keep my eyes on him for now.

After counseling, I asked Jill if I could call home but she drummed up some excuse about how no one was able to make any phone calls on Thursdays.

"Why the hell can't we make any calls on Thursdays?" I'd asked. She made up the most bullcrap excuse as to why no one was able to phone home on Mondays, Wednesdays, or Thursdays. I then asked why she'd told me yesterday that I'd be able to call home today. She told me she'd forgotten that rule and was reminded about it today. Apparently it was her first year working at Palisades and she was still kind of new. For some reason, I didn't really believe her. It seemed like she was trying to pull a fast one on me and making up senseless rules on a whim.

At dinner, I scanned the cafeteria and searched for the big girl that had been taken away earlier that morning, but I failed to locate her. I also didn't see Helen. I was beginning to get worried. My mind sometimes goes into these dark places and I start making up outlandish scenarios, and thinking up crazy stuff.

Maybe, I thought, those girls were taken to a screening room and forced to stare at ultra-violent images, like Alex in

A Clockwork Orange. Eyes pried open and forced to stare at horrific images, in an attempt to force them to behave and conform. The *Ludovico Treatment.* I love that movie. Pat, Doug, and I had watched it several times.

But no sign of the girls. They'd vanished. I wanted to ask Chatterbox what she thought happened to Helen and the big girl, but I was afraid that once I'd ask her, I'd open up a can of worms and she'd never stop yapping.

Well, that's about all I have for you today. It was a relatively boring day. I asked about calling my parents tomorrow and they told me that they'd allow it, since tomorrow is Friday. They'd better let me call home. I need to talk to my dad and try to convince him to let me out of this hellhole. I have a better shot at convincing him than Mom. My mom has it out for me. We've always had a sort of coarse relationship. She thinks I'm nuts. But I know I'm still daddy's little girl. I just have to get him on the line. I *know* I can convince him. All right. I'm gonna hide my journal now and get some sleep. Peace.

JULY 3

Dear Diary,

Helen's back. And so is the big girl. I saw them both at breakfast. There's something *off* about them, though. It's hard to tell at first with Helen because she's so quiet all the time. I noticed there was something different, something strange, about her during counseling. She wore a vacant look, as if she wasn't completely all there.

Chatterbox and I were lazing out in the courtyard when I asked her whether she noticed something different about Helen. But as soon as I did, I knew I'd made a big mistake. She completely dodged my question, and went on a long rant about how *we have to make sure to behave, because if we don't, we'll end up in the Safe Room, and that's not conducive to our recovery.* She was very expressive when she spoke, her eyes opened wide, and her mouth flapped real ugly-like. She reminded me of a trout caught on a fishing line. I should probably add that she's pretty dowdy, and these quirks made her even less attractive.

God, I think she just likes the sound of her own voice. I was so frustrated that she couldn't answer a damned simple question. I wanted to clock her right then and there, but I restrained myself. I was trying really hard to not get into any fights. I'd been able to reign in my anger thus far. Hell, maybe I've turned over a new leaf.

When I saw Jill, I turned and left Chatterbox, blabbering away to the air. I couldn't bear her long-winded speeches anymore. They were becoming didactic. I swear, I was ready to pop her right on her mouth, but I knew the moment I got into an altercation, my chances of going home would be null and void.

Didactic's a cool word. I remember learning it in English class when I was at the Catholic school. It means to teach a lesson or a moral. As much as I hate school, I do enjoy learning new words. It makes me feel like I'm smart when I use them, even though I know I'm not book smart.

Anyway, back to Helen and the big girl. Helen was extra quiet during counseling. She didn't share out at all today. I wanted to talk to her to try to find out where they'd taken her, but I never got the opportunity. I was afraid to bring it up in front of Jack and Jill. Something is up with this place. It doesn't take a rocket scientist to figure that out. The counselors, the staff, the people who run the joint, even the janitors, all seem odd. Everyone here seems a little *culty*. I really need to make that call home, the more I think about it.

I saw the big girl throughout the day. Like Helen, she also walked around with a vacant glaze in her eyes. Like there was nothing firing up there anymore. Where had these girls been taken? What did they do to them? The mystery was really starting to gnaw at me.

They finally let me call home after dinner. They said I had five minutes to talk, which sounds like a lot of time, but five minutes flies by when you're trying to convince your dad of something important.

My dad picked up the phone after three rings.

"Hi hon," he said. "How have you been holding up at Palisades?"

"Dad—" I got right into it, "—you've gotta let me come home. Please." I was trying to whisper so the staff wouldn't hear me. I glanced over to my right. The screw who was escorting me stood only ten feet away, peering toward me, narrowing his eyes at me. "Please dad," I went on. "I don't like this place. The girls here suck. I promise, I'll behave if you let me come home," I said, whispering, giving it my all.

"I'm sorry, sweetheart, but you've got to stay there. You only just got there three days ago," he said. "You have to stay for a while to work on your anger. They can teach you how to manage it better and I'm sure you can learn a lot of other things while you're there." He paused for a moment. "Palisades has a great reputation. It's got stellar reviews. They've helped a lot of young girls who have gone through similar challenges."

"Please dad—"

"Hon," he cut me off. "There's something I need to tell you." He sighed. "One of the main reasons your mother and I decided to send you there—"

My heart started jackhammering. I knew that whatever he was about to say was going to ruin my night. Possibly my entire week.

"Your mother's cancer is back. The doctors saw something on her last scan and when they tested it… well…"

I was trying so hard to suppress the tears that were doing their damn best to break through, like an old levee trying to keep the water out during a powerful hurricane.

"They broke the news to us at her last appointment two weeks ago," he went on.

The lump in my throat was like a giant golf ball.

"We figured it was better, sweetheart," he continued, "if you were away for a little while so mom could go back to getting her treatments and try to recover." I could hear him taking deep breaths on the line. I was sure he didn't want to be telling me all this over the phone, but he had to. He had no other choice. Who knew when we'd see each other again. Visitations were apparently limited during the first few weeks of treatment. "She could do better without all the stress," he finally said.

"I'm so sorry, dad," was all I could muster. My eyes welled up. "I miss you and mom."

When I looked up, the screw in charge of the telephones hovered right over me, practically breathing on me. He pried the phone from my hand and said, "Your five minutes is up," and slammed the phone back on the cradle.

He grabbed me by my arm and led me out of the office.

I wanted to turn and ram my fist right into his face. There was that fury I sometimes felt, that red anger that had gotten me into so much trouble in the past, percolating through my skin. Sparks of electricity buzzed through my marrow. But it quickly dissipated and went away. It left my body, leaving me feeling empty and doleful. My poor mother. She'd been through so much in the last couple of years. We were ecstatic when we heard she was in remission. My dad threw a party for her and we invited a few close relatives and some of her best friends. And now it's back. WTF?! Today is like the worst day ever. Being stuck in here doesn't make it any better. We usually have free time after dinner, but I didn't feel like socializing in the common room tonight after I'd heard the news. I just came back to my room and I've been laying in bed, thinking, brooding, and now writing. I feel wiped after my dad dropped that bomb on me. I'm going to close my eyes and try to get some sleep. Maybe if I sleep a long time, I'll feel a little better tomorrow. I'm signing off now. Peace.

JULY 4

Dear Diary,

Today is Independence Day and I can't believe I'm not home, hanging out with Pat and Doug. Last year, we pooled our money together and bought a bunch of fireworks. We fired off Roman candles, ground spinners, firecrackers, and this giant multi-shot cake that went off for like two whole minutes straight. It was fucking spectacular. God bless America. Towards the end of our lightshow, Pat blew up an M-1000. That's a quarter stick of dynamite for all you geezers. We were about a hundred feet away from it when it went off, and my ears were ringing for a long while afterwards. The cops arrived soon after we set it off and we had to dip. Luckily, we had our bikes, and there's no way the piggies were catching us on those. We've memorized all the shortcuts around town and can go up one-way streets.

Unfortunately, this year's Independence Day was much more low-key. It was flat out boring. The staff organized a soiree for us out in the courtyard. The cooks barbecued hot dogs and hamburgers for everyone. The burgers were okay, except they'd gotten Ball Park Franks hot dogs. What I'd like to know is who was the psychopath who made that decision? Everyone knows you have to go Nathan's or Sabrett. Anything else is just blasphemy. They decorated the outdoor tables with American flag table cloths, and set out American flag themed napkins, cups, and the likes. I just hate being treated like a little kid. There was even a DJ, but the bozo played Kidz Bop. Christ almighty. Most of us here are in our late teens, not eight years-old.

I should probably mention I met a new girl today. I actually went out of my comfort zone and talked to someone besides the three girls in my counseling group. I made it a point to try to not interact with too many of these loonies when I first got here, but this girl seems pretty chill. Her name is Bex, short for Rebecca. Pretty cool name if you ask me. She's apparently trans. Whatever the hell that means. I'm not too keen on what people identify as these days. Maybe if I get to know her a little better, I'll ask her what that's all about.

Bex had a flower in her hair, and that somehow told me she was cool.

I sat near her and started up the conversation. I looked around to make sure there were no staff around who could listen in. We were grabbing a burger and I waited until we were far away enough that none of the screws would hear us. "This might sound like a weird question," I said, "but, would you happen to know where I might be able to find some weed."

Bex turned toward me and smiled. *Come on*, I thought. A girl with a flower in her hair *has* to know where to find some.

"As a matter of fact, I do," she said. "It'll cost you, though."

"Do you accept IOUs?" I asked. "They took all my money during intake, and since we're not allowed to have our phones, I can't exactly send you any on Digicoin."

She laughed. "Listen," she said, "You seem pretty chill." She glanced around quickly, checking to see if any screws were nearby eavesdropping on our conversation. When the coast seemed clear, she continued, "I'll share some with you, but not here. We have to be real careful, cause if we get caught —" she stopped and gave me a worried look. She seemed afraid to say the words out loud, as if saying them would somehow conjure those creepy security guards out of thin air.

I waited for a moment, eager for her to finish telling me. When I realized she wasn't going to say anything else, I asked, "What would happen if we were to get caught?"

"If anyone gets caught smoking weed, it would be really, really bad," she said. "You'd be sent to the Safe Room for a long time."

"I keep hearing about the Safe Room. What is that place?"

She leaned in close, and said, "You don't ever want to go to the Safe Room. I mean ever." Her soft smile had completely evaporated now, replaced by a stony expression. Then she said, in a voice that was much too loud, "You understand me?"

I jerked back, startled by her tone.

"You do whatever the fuck you can to never get sent there," she added.

My imagination was running wild when Batgirl came over and hijacked our conversation.

"Do they think we're little children?" Batgirl said, waving her hand toward the other girls, who were engaged in admittedly, childish games of one form or another. "They're playing pin the tail on the donkey. Can this place get any more lame?"

"What would you rather be doing?" Bex asked her.

"Seriously? Anything else," Batgirl muttered. "Spin the bottle."

Bex laughed and said, "I don't see any boys around."

"So…"

I glanced from Bex to Batgirl and suddenly got an uncomfortable feeling in my gut. I felt like a third wheel, intruding on some private joke.

Bex smiled. "You're such a slut, you know that?"

"I know," Batgirl admitted, then squealed, laughing maniacally, like Harley Quinn.

Bex moved in closer toward us and whispered, "After all the food's done, they'll let us play games for about another forty-five minutes, maybe an hour." Her tone sounded like she was plotting a bank robbery. Leaning in some more, she added, "This is what we'll do—we'll go for a walk around the track—" she pointed toward it, "and when we're at the far end, we'll each take a few hits from my vape."

I couldn't believe what I was hearing. Leaning in, I whispered, "You have a vape?"

How the hell did she manage to smuggle that in with her? I wondered. They nearly performed a body cavity check on me during intake. She must have a magician's skills. I knew asking questions wasn't the smart thing to do (I was afraid someone would overhear our plan), so I just let it go, and accepted Bex was just one very crafty girl. I knew she'd be someone cool to talk to, and dammit, I was right. We were finally going to have a little bit of fun and let loose.

We played a game of cornhole so as to not seem so conspicuous, then we trailed off in the direction of the track as nonchalantly as possible.

Just as we were breaking away from the group, Chatterbox appeared out of nowhere. *She's like a goddamn leech*, I thought.

"Where are you all going?" she asked.

I groaned and Bex gave me a funny look.

When Bex greeted her, I realized she must be clueless as to how annoying Chatterbox was and how she never stopped talking.

"We're gonna walk around the track for a little while before we have to go back in," Batgirl said. "Wanna join?"

No! You idiot. Why would you…

"Chatterbox, I was talking to Bex about something," I said, "Why don't you give us a moment so we can—"

"It's cool," Bex cut in. "You can come with us."

Dammit.

She tagged along despite my evident displeasure. I didn't like the feel of this. There were too many of us now, I thought, and we would all be weirdly walking around the track, and possibly drawing too much attention to ourselves.

I took a deep breath, and sighed. I looked toward the sun. It was sinking near the horizon, and it would be dark in less than an hour. Then I glanced back toward the party. The screws seemed to be busy cooking, managing the games, chatting with some of the girls and amongst themselves.

"Okay, just don't be a buzzkill," I warned her.

We walked, side by side, along the track. When we got to the far end, Bex took a quick pull from her vape then passed it to me. I turned away from the building and courtyard, and took two quick hits. I passed it to Batgirl. She took a hit and started coughing. She stopped and bent over, continuing to cough like a goddamn rookie. I took the vape from her and slid it in my pocket. We all huddled around her, checking to see if she was okay. She raised her head and her eyes looked glassy.

"I'm all right," she assured us, then we continued on.

As we neared the party, I glanced toward the staff and counselors. Some of them looked over at us but they didn't seem too interested in what we were doing. I couldn't believe we were getting away with it.

We walked around the track a total of three times, and took more tokes from the vape when we were on the far end, away from everyone. After our last lap, I was feeling pretty good. The sun was nearly setting and I could feel goosebumps prickling all over my skin. I tend to get a little cold when I smoke pot. I'm not a pothead, or anything like that. Back home, Pat and Doug and I rarely smoke pot. We drink sometimes, but our main forms of entertainment are looking for fun stuff to do—normal things teenagers do. Ride our bikes real fast down steep hills, shoot Pat's BB gun, go paintballing, watch old movies (Escape From Alcatraz is one of my favorites!), and sneak into the cemetery after dark. Those sorta things. But here, at the Auschwitz Girls Reformatory, finding out Bex had a vape turned out to be a great diversion. Something to prevent me from losing my head.

Anyway, it's almost legal in all fifty states. And, why not smoke a little loud on America's birthday. To America, land of the free. Even though I'm not free at all, and actually confined with a bunch of loonies. Well, I'm getting tired. I've been writing in the girls' bathroom and I'm going to leave my diary hidden in one of the panels in the drop ceiling. Bex had told me that the staff randomly search our rooms from time to time, so she hides her vape and other paraphernalia in secret hiding spots around the Academy. I figured it might be a good idea for me to do that too, if I don't want anyone to get a hold of my diary, especially after I've written so much about this place. Okay. I'm gonna hide it now and hit the hay. Be back to tell you more about my adventures (or misadventures) at the Palisades Girls Academy tomorrow. Peace out.

JULY 5

Dear Diary,

Bex is gone. She might've been taken to the Safe Room, but no one really knows for sure.

It all started at the butt crack of dawn. Actually, the sun wasn't even up yet. It was probably four in the morning when the clamor began, if I had to guess. I'm not a hundred percent sure because they don't allow us to have clocks or watches on us. The lights were thrust on and before I knew it, there was staff and security at our door, yelling at the top of their lungs.

It took me a few seconds to figure out what was going on. It was all happening so abruptly, so quickly, and everything seemed so confusing and muddled at that hour.

Then, suddenly, when I rolled and faced the door, I saw a security guard's big head yelling into the glass window. His face was beet red and his mouth flapped angrily like Gunnery Sergeant Hartman in *Full Metal Jacket*. "SHAKEDOWN, LADIES! GET OUT OF BED, AND STAND IN THE CENTER OF YOUR ROOM!" He banged on the door. "Don't touch or pick anything up. Just stand in the center!"

It reminded me of those prison shows I'd seen on Netflix, and I couldn't believe it was happening to me.

When I turned, I saw Chatterbox's legs dangling from her bunk. She shimmied off and plopped on the ground.

I slid out of bed and shielded my eyes from the light. It was so damn bright and I wasn't ready for it. The alarms were so painfully loud, they hurt my ears. I remember I'd been having a dream just before I woke up. I can't recall the exact details of the dream but I remember it being a pleasant one. So much for finally feeling like I was getting a good night's sleep. A tall, slim guard barged in and began raiding our room. He stripped the sheets from the mattresses and ransacked our drawers.

Thank god I hid my journal in the bathroom last night, I reminded myself.

"Out of the room!" the big, burly guard shouted, prodding us out. The slimmer man remained inside, continuing to search the room. "Let's go, move it! Move it!" he shouted.

From the hallway, I could hear the other screw knocking things around and being rough with our belongings. We didn't have much in terms of possessions, but I felt the anger rising inside of me.

This isn't prison, I thought. *Why the hell are they messing with our stuff? Why are they fucking searching our rooms? And at this hour?*

"On the floor!" the fat guard yelled, his spittle flying in my face. "On your stomach!"

I dropped down to the floor like I was getting ready to do push-ups.

A crackly voice—a woman's and one I'd never heard before—came on through the loudspeakers. "Girls, please follow directions and do as you're told."

The guard patted me down, and actually touched me in places where I didn't want to be touched—where I'd never imagined being touched by an adult—especially by an old creep. I wanted to scream.

"Understand that this procedure is solely for your welfare —" the voice over the speakers continued, "ensuring an optimal and swift recovery. Failure to cooperate without delay will lead to immediate and severe consequences."

The guard patted my butt, his hand lingering longer than necessary. I wanted to turn around and spit in his face. I'd never felt so wronged in my entire life. I almost did, but then the wailing alarms subsided and the guard hoisted me up off the ground, and told me to return to my room.

When I turned, I saw Chatterbox was being taken away.

I wanted to yell out but I swallowed the desire, feeling

powerless and fearing what would happen if I did. My eyes welled with tears and I mustered all the energy I could to stop them from pouring out. I didn't want those screws to know they'd gotten to me. I'd been here just six days, and the last thing I wanted to do was admit defeat or show them they'd broken me. But that's exactly how I felt. Broken like a mirror that had been tossed from a second story. I felt a pulsing surge of fury course through me, aching to be released.

I sat down on my bed and pulled my knees to my chest, hugging them tight. After the screw had finally left my room, I began to cry.

The rest of the morning through counseling, was mostly a blur. I was angry and sad and sort of in a fugue state. I kept wondering where they'd taken Chatterbox. I just had lunch and I'm taking a bathroom break now. I wanted to get all this stuff written down in my diary while it's still fresh in my mind.

There's an intense rage bubbling inside me, and I'm not sure I'll be able to hold it in for much longer. It reminds me of all those times just before I'd gotten into fights, and then I'd let my fists go flying. I want to scream. In my head, I'm screaming my head off.

AHHHHHHHH!!

I can't outwardly scream because if I do, I'm afraid they'll take me to the Safe Room. That dreaded room is still a mystery. I need to get to the bottom of it. I have a feeling it's tied to all the weirdness that goes on around here.

I have to talk to my dad. I'm sure I can convince him, somehow. If he just lets me come home, I swear to him I'll be good. I won't give my parents anymore trouble. Not anymore. Not ever. I'll behave. Get a job. Help them out—especially Mom. I'll manage her appointments, her meds—everything and anything she needs. I just need to make the call.

Okay. I gotta go. I have to go to meditation at two o'clock. I'm realizing this place is more Christian camp—more culty— than I'd originally realized. But I'll tell you about that later (maybe tonight), when I'm able to write some more. Peace out.

JULY 9

Dear Diary,

I was sent to the Safe Room for three days.

I can't write for too long. There's a guard waiting outside the girls' bathroom. He escorted me here (my personal chaperone. Lucky me!), and I'm afraid if I'm in here for too long, they'll come in and find me writing in my journal.

Here's what happened.

That day, I'd been feeling pretty sad about learning my mom's cancer had come back. I was also pissed the hell off about the security guard groping my private parts at four in the morning. The more the day wore on, the angrier I got.

I'd been minding my own business at dinner when a girl I'd never talked to commented on my hair.

I was waiting in line to get served lunch. My back was turned and I tried to ignore her, hoping she'd get bored and go away. Or maybe pick on someone else.

"I asked you a question," the girl pressed.

I ignored her.

"Did you hear what I said, dyke?" she snapped at me. "What's with the haircut? You a lesbo or something?"

That's all it took.

I whipped around, cocked my arm back, and hurled my fist directly at her nose. It landed right on target. I felt her nose crunch. It felt like I'd hit a thick T-Bone steak. Pain shot through my knuckles and wrist, and all the way down to my forearm. It might've been the hardest I'd ever punched anyone in my entire life.

The girl's legs buckled and her hands went up to her face. Almost instantly, a gusher of blood sprayed out through her nose. It reminded me of when kids laugh so hard while drinking milk and the liquid spouts out through their smeller.

This was similar, except it was a thick stream of red shooting out her nostrils.

Security jumped on me pretty quickly after I'd punched the girl's lights out. As I was being carried away, I saw her group of friends looking pale and horrified, as if they were watching Carrie in the flesh. They'd probably never seen anything like it. They didn't even move a finger to help their bitch of a friend up or anything. They just stood there, terror-stricken, with thumbs up their asses. Standing like statues, gasping.

That's why I was sent to the Safe Room. I'm going to hide my diary now and flush the toilet. I don't want to be here for too long, otherwise it'll seem suspicious. I'll try to come back tomorrow and write about what it was like. Just a few days ago, I wanted to get out of here because I was bored and thought I didn't belong here with these crazies. Now, I'm seriously scared something might happen to me. Something really, *really* bad, and I need to figure out how to get out of here. Be back soon. Peace.

Dear Diary,

The Safe Room is not what I expected.

I literally pictured a white room with padded walls. Possibly a thick, metal door, with a small shatterproof window.

Nope. That's not what it was at all.

After I punched the girl out, and security lugged me out of the cafeteria, I was taken through a maze of hallways until I ended up in an area of Palisades I'd never seen before. I hadn't realized how big the Academy was until I was dragged through the property.

When we'd been outside in the courtyard, I never really bothered to take a good look at the facility. The building itself was three stories tall and much larger than I'd originally thought. It seemed like there were hidden corridors that twisted and turned. You wouldn't expect the place to be designed like that if you were just looking at it from the outside.

I was taken to a small room at first, which I had mistaken for being the Safe Room. The room was gray with blindingly bright lights. Even though I wasn't totally sure, I figured the mirror that covered an entire side of the room was a two-way mirror. It felt like there were eyes on me, peering in from the other side.

Once inside the room, the screws tossed me in and locked the door. I was there for about an hour.

While waiting, I wondered if they would beat me for my sins and transgressions. Maybe they'd discipline the last bit of defiance out of me with switches.

After an hour had passed, a nurse entered.

She wore a bone white V-neck and matching scrub pants.

"Strip," she ordered.

Once I'd slipped into the hospital gown she handed me, she stuck out her palm, revealing two large white pills.

"Take these."

I stared at the pills and shook my head. I had stopped crying at that point, but I was exhausted. I'd fought the guards the entire way there, kicking and flailing, bucking under their firm grasp, attempting to escape. I'm surprised they didn't strike me, the way I'd acted.

"Please, Sue. Make things easy on yourself," the nurse said, raising the pills up toward my mouth. "If you resist, we'll have to administer the medication through a different means." She hesitated for a moment, sighed, then said, "I'd have to administer it by means of injection. Would you rather me use a syringe?"

I shook my head and muttered, "No," then reached out and took the pills from her.

Who in the hell knew what they were. I put them in my mouth but didn't swallow.

She handed me a small cup of water.

I didn't want my mind to be dulled, unable to act accordingly and defend myself if the situation called for it.

I then had another miserable thought. What would they do to me if they found out I hadn't swallowed the pills?

After placing them in my mouth, I pretended to swallow, but instead I used my tongue to navigate the meds to the side. I prayed that if they were to check my mouth, make me say *ahhh,* they wouldn't see them.

Thinking back on it now, I'm not sure that was the wisest idea. I'm trying not to think of what happened next—of what I experienced. I'd find out later the pills were, in fact, to dull my mind.

Anyway, it's probably best I write down in great detail what happened next, in case something bad happens to me. I need this journal to serve as my record in case things go awry here in this hellhole.

The nurse made me say *ahh* and once she seemed satisfied I'd ingested the pills (I must've done a good job at hiding them), she left the room.

About five minutes passed when the two guards (the same ones who dragged me into the room), came in and grabbed a hold of me. Guards on each arm, they marched me past a row of closed doors and dumped me into another sterile room. The walls here were hospital white, the floor a relentless mosaic of tile. A mirror spanned the length of one wall. Another two-way, I assumed.

The room looked unassuming, similar to the prior one I'd been in, except there was a restraint chair, and a cutting-edge machine that looked like it belonged in an ophthalmologist's office. That's the best way I could describe it. A pair of VR goggles were attached to its framework with cables.

This new room *was* the Safe Room. I'm pretty sure it was, anyway. It was the last room I remember being dragged to.

Sweat trickled down my forehead and the back of my neck. My palms felt clammy. My gaze fixed itself on the machine. Wires trailed out of it like silicone tendrils. Dread began to spread through me like a tightening coil. Trying hard not to seem suspicious (since I hadn't swallowed the pills), I did my best to play it cool. I figured I had to play along with their little farce so I could get out of there as quickly as possible and be placed back in gen pop.

I kept my breathing steady while the guards handed me over to a new set of nurses. Their faces were anonymous behind masks and scrubs, strangers I'd never seen in all my time at the academy. This is a much bigger operation than I'd originally suspected. It felt as though I was being prepared for surgery. Glancing around the room, though, I didn't glimpse an operating table or any surgical tools. I probably would've freaked if I had seen any scalpels or bone saws.

Two nurses ushered me toward the machine and sat me down on the chair that looked like it belonged in an asylum.

One of the nurses attached small electrodes to my head. Once she'd finished attaching them, the other nurse pulled the VR goggles over my eyes. I went semi-limp in their grasp, pretending I was out of it, as they maneuvered me, allowing them to guide me in any direction they wished. My acting seemed to work because they didn't think anything of it— they didn't question my docility.

Small earbuds were lodged in each of my ears, and then soft outer shells were placed over them. They felt like earmuffs, and I'd guess their purpose was to prevent the earbuds from getting loose and falling out of my ears.

Once the nurses had positioned me onto the device, I began to see the images. They were black and white at first, like from a classic movie, except they seemed very real, documentary-like, and three-dimensional.

The images that flashed in front of my retinas were deeply religious. One sequence I remember vividly reenacted Christ carrying the cross. The Procession to Calvary. That prominent scene was etched in my mind from Sunday school.

Then, suddenly, I was in a white-tiled room. It looked like the Safe Room but I didn't see a mirror anywhere. The tiles began to separate and float apart, revealing a black chasm.

There was a man with an oppressive presence drifting behind the floating tiles. They were separating and moving about with weightlessness. It was difficult to see him as he stood in the gloom beyond the tiles, masked in deep shadows. I wanted to ask him who he was, but I was so afraid I couldn't move my mouth to speak. The room felt icy cold and I trembled, shrinking back in fear. In a low, guttural voice, the man said, "If he is really the king of the Jews, he can save himself!"

Then, it was as if fingers began to dig themselves into my brain. My head radiated with slicing pain. My brain felt like it was being unspooled—a clinical, rhythmic flaying of the cortex that made the concept of a headache seem like a childish complaint from a world that had ceased to exist.

I cried out, begging for the pain to stop. But it didn't stop. The pain got more pronounced, more extreme.

As the room fractured and the man emerged from the gloom, I finally got a clear look at his features. What I saw startled me worse than any nightmare I'd ever experienced. His face was mutilated beyond the most deranged person's imagination. His teeth were muck-black, broken down to jagged angles, and his tongue, which was forked like a snake's, slithered out through them. He held a crown of barbed-wire. Blood dripped from the galvanized points. As he approached me, I realized he intended to place the crown on my head. I shrieked and backed up into a wall. With nowhere to go, I began to cry. *Christ almighty, get me out of here.*

Then everything went black and I saw what looked like computer code flash for a millisecond. The VR goggles were detached from my face and I was back in the white room.

My head was spinning when I returned and I felt impossibly dizzy. It took me half a minute to adjust to my surroundings. One of the nurses stuck an ophthalmoscope in front of my face.

"I have to throw up," I cautioned, trying not to get sick on her.

"Bring that over here," she told another nurse, pointing to a bucket in the corner. Before I knew it, I was slumped over barfing. After what seemed like an eternity, there was nothing left to expel, and I dry-heaved for a time.

My brain felt squeezed inward, my skull suddenly too small to contain the massive surge of pressure it had just undergone.

I felt out of breath and struggled to fill my lungs with air.

It felt so real. So frighteningly real, I thought afterwards.

How did they know? When I was in the second grade, my

Sunday school teacher had taught us about The Procession to Calvary. It had really freaked me out, and apparently it was still a trigger.

An intense hopelessness lingered and my head hurt like bloody hell for the rest of the evening. Maybe I might've felt different if I had taken those pills. Better I hadn't in the end and faced the consequences. But would it have been better if I'd taken them?

The pills.

I still had them hidden in my mouth when I was taken out of the Safe Room and was ushered to a rubber room (where I stayed during the remainder of my time in isolation). Inside the room, there was a small cot and a toilet. The pills had dissolved a bit. I cupped them in my right palm, covertly, and sat on the toilet. As I wiped, I dropped them between my legs and flushed. I was probably being watched through a camera. This place *must* have cameras secretly placed along the perimeters of every corridor and every room. Everywhere I went, it felt like there were eyes on me.

I didn't see any of the other girls during my stint in the Safe Room. I only interacted with a couple of nurses, a doctor (who never introduced himself), and a few stone-faced screws.

I don't know if I'm doing a good job describing what I'd experienced, but that's what happened there in a nutshell.

The sessions on the machine the next two days were horrible.

The following day, as I settled into that hospital-ward chair, I braced myself for the man with the black teeth. He never showed. For that, I was grateful.

As I settled in and the goggles were lowered over my eyes, the sensations were far more intense than the day before. It began with blasts of heat scorching my face and body. I found myself in an expansive red landscape, something like a Martian desert. There were low, jagged, rust-red cliffs with fires cresting nearly everywhere I looked. I turned my head and saw a river that flowed not with water, but with red lava, sludging along lazily as smoke billowed from floating embers into a blighted sky.

I began to cough and choke on the thick air, which was heavily saturated with ash and soot. It became difficult, virtually impossible to breathe. My eyes burned and I shut them, shielding them from the scorching atmosphere.

When I opened my eyes again, I began to see *them*.

The creatures.

I don't know what they were, but they were short and stubby and had fat, round torsos, and ears that spiked into horns at the ends. They were bald on top—their skulls gleamed with perspiration in the scarlet sun. Their eyes were black pools, bottomless and heavy with a primitive malice.

They began to bleat, in unison: "For the wages of sin is death! For the wages of sin is death!"

Over and over again, they cried out the phrase, like a broken record. Their discordant voices were unbearable. I tried cupping my hands over my ears, but their cries bled right through.

"Stop it," I yelled. "Stop!"

I ran from them as fast as I could. My lungs burned. It felt like I was running inside an oven set on broil.

I glanced back to see the pack closing in. Several of them were swinging spiked steel flails, the chains rattling against their clubs as the heavy balls whistled through the air.

At one point, I collapsed onto the red-hot sand and broke out into a sob.

I don't want to even remember it, it was so horrible.

The goggles were stripped away, and I was sick for a long time. I ended up sprawled on the floor of the Safe Room, clutching the bucket like a lifeline while my stomach burned as if I'd ingested battery acid.

I was so tired and battered.

When I spat the pills out, the nurses saw I hadn't taken them—that I'd been hiding them in my mouth the entire time.

One of them jabbed me with a syringe. Everything was hazy and dreamlike after the shot.

They brought me back to my original room early this morning. Chatterbox didn't even slam me with a million questions. She must've known where I'd been; she quickly picked up that I was out of sorts and not in the mood to stomach her usual rigmarole. Word had most likely gotten around already about my stint in the Safe Room. Either way, I was grateful she didn't chew my ear off when I returned. I was recovering from the experience—in fact, I still am.

I never thought I'd say this, but I'm glad to be back in my old room, and I'm actually glad to be back with Chatterbox. I was so alone over there.

God, the Safe Room was fucking awful. Every time I think about it I get sick to my stomach. I *need* to get out of here. I truly feel that if I'm here for much longer, I might just lose it. I *can't* go back there.

If my parents plan to keep me here for an extended period of time, maybe I'll have to plan to escape. Hey, if Frank Morris escaped freakin' Alcatraz, I think I might have a shot of escaping The Palisades *Hellhole* Academy.

I'm going to put my diary away now. When I leave the bathroom, I'm thinking I'll tell the security guard that I got sick, and that's why I was in the bathroom for so long. It's partly true, since I still feel like crap. All right. I'm gonna head back and hopefully get some sleep. I need to get these awful thoughts out of my head and maybe if I'm lucky, I can sleep it off. I'll be back tomorrow (hopefully). Peace out.

Dear Diary,

I didn't sleep well last night. I had awful nightmares. I think they were aftershocks of what I'd experienced in the Safe Room. I feel as though those images were somehow burned into my brain.

Was it a nightmare or something I remember from my stint in the Safe Room? To tell you the truth, now I'm not too sure.

Anyway, the nightmare I'm trying to erase from my mind began like this: I was walking in a sea of naked people—old, young, middle-aged.

A girl slightly older than me, who walked with a lurching gait, turned toward me and said, "We're going to shower now. We need to be cleansed."

I tried not to look at her body. She was emaciated. She must've been about five foot six and weighed only fifty pounds soaking wet.

I couldn't get out from the hoard of people. I was flanked and wedged in between a sea of gaunt people. The throng moved toward a door with a metal lever on top, and another on the bottom.

A military officer dressed in all black, donning a cap with an eagle, pulled the door open and shouted *"Innen!"* He waved his hand, directing everyone inside. The pallid crowd careened in, shoving me deep into the room.

A few elderly people collapsed as soon as they entered; others attempted to walk around them, but many trampled them, unable to sidestep due to the impasse.

I held onto the young girl's hand.

"Where are we?" I asked, my voice trembling.

I was naked, too, but didn't feel embarrassed. There

seemed to be far greater things to worry about. I shuddered. It was as cold as a meat locker.

"Don't be afraid," the girl said to me, smiling. "It's only a shower."

Then I woke up.

I don't know how much more of this I can take.

It's mentally exhausting.

I'm trying to write it all down and do it quickly because I can't spend too much time in the bathroom.

So, that was the last Safe Room session I remember. I need to cut to what happened in counseling today. Helen wasn't there. Chatterbox was surprisingly quiet, and so was Batgirl, who usually has something to say.

Jack and Jill's smiles looked even bigger and wider than how I'd remembered them. Their grins looked maniacal, like an evil clown who'd just gotten away with carrying out mischief at a carnival.

Jill had a Bible out on her lap and read us some passages from a scripture. Smiling, she said, "Do not be overcome by evil, but overcome evil with good."

Then, Chatterbox cut in: "For there is no authority except from God, and those that exist have been instituted by God."

Oh, my god, I thought. *She's drank the fucking Kool-Aid.*

I spotted Bex in the cafeteria during lunchtime that afternoon. Although I wasn't completely sure, I had a hunch that maybe she'd been sent to the Safe Room, since she'd disappeared right before I was taken away.

I sat next to her after I grabbed my lunch.

"Hi-ya, Bex," I said.

"Hey," she answered, turning her eyes toward me, then glancing away.

"You okay?" I asked.

She seemed different. She was *definitely* taken to the Safe Room, I thought. Same as me.

"Where'd they take you?" I got right to it. I didn't want to waste any time, wanting to compare my experience with hers. "Did they put you on the machine?"

She looked confused.

"What machine?"

"The VR machine," I said. "The Safe Room machine. You know—"

"I'm not sure what you're talking about," she said, keeping her voice low. "I was taken to the Safe Room… but there was no machine. I don't want to talk about it."

I wasn't sure how to respond. *No machine.* Where did they take her?

"Listen," I whispered, placing my hand over hers. "We need to get out of here. I'm going to try to escape. Come with me."

Bex jerked her head toward me and she opened her eyes wide. "Sue…" she whispered, swiveling around, checking to see if there were any staff or security eavesdropping nearby. "There's no escaping. There's no getting out. They got us locked up like wards in a modern-day gulag."

I opened my mouth, searching for a rebuttal, but I couldn't find one. "What's a gulag?" was all I could think of.

She just shook her head, then continued eating her lunch. We both sat in silence for a while.

Bex had so much charisma, so much pizzazz just a few days ago. Now, all of that had vanished. If she hadn't been taken to the Safe Room, where had they taken her? I wondered what else was hidden behind those heavy metal doors.

This place is completely fucked. I am beginning to lose my mind. Not only were they messing with us physically, but they were meddling with our psyches, and if no one else wants to try to get out of here, I'll have to do it alone.

JULY 12

Dear Diary,

I think I've figured out how I'm going to get out of here—
how I'm going to escape.

They allow us forty-five minutes of rec time every day,
and when I was outside earlier, I strolled around the track a
few times. I did a pretty good job taking mental notes of the
facility's layout. There's a tall security gate that surrounds the
entire backside of the complex. The courtyard faces the gate,
the eastern side, and I spotted where the cameras are located.
If I could get out here in the middle of the night somehow,
and circumvent the security cameras, I should be able to run
toward the gate and hop it. There isn't barbed wire or
anything like that lining the top, so it's nothing I can't handle.
I just need to figure out how I'm going to leave my room in
the middle of the night and get through a few doors without
anyone noticing.

What would Frank Morris do? I had to think like an expert
criminal—like an escape artist. This wouldn't be an easy feat.
They were keeping a close watch on everyone, but after my
stint in the Safe Room, the paranoia felt different. They were
definitely tracking me. The more I think about it, the more I
realize we're being monitored like inmates. Calling this a *therapeutic boarding school* felt like a cheap, transparent front.

I'm going to put my journal down now. I need to knuckle
down and spend the rest of the day plotting my escape carefully. I'm thinking maybe I'll leave tonight. Godspeed.

JULY 13

Dear Diary,

Last night went horribly.

I set out early in the morning, but never made it out.

Here's what happened and why I returned.

I stayed up very late last night, playing possum in my bunk, until I decided it was time to attempt my escape. It must've been around two in the morning when I finally crept out of bed and snuck out of the room.

Chatterbox was fast asleep, snoring like an English Bulldog.

The dorms and hallways were eerily silent. Usually, I'm asleep by nine-thirty, ten o'clock at the latest since we wake up so early. It felt strange lurking around the facility so late without any supervision or anyone around.

A thought suddenly crossed my mind, as I lurked down the dark corridor. *Where did the staff and counselors sleep?* Did they reside in the facility, or did they commute to work? I'd never given it much thought until then. Like, who actually stayed in the facility overnight?

I didn't see any screws, but just because they were nowhere to be seen didn't mean they weren't around a bend, waiting to pounce on me.

I tried to blend in with the shadows, tip-toeing through the corridor that led to the back of the facility. From there I could find an exit that led to the courtyard.

I was really starting to map this place out.

Once I'd turned a corner, I saw the hallway that led toward the Safe Room. *Never again*, I thought.

I was about to dash down the opposite way, when I heard some strange noises. At first, it sounded like a television.

I stopped midway down the hallway and turned, facing the direction the sounds were traveling from.

I hesitated for a moment, then took a deep breath and headed toward the Safe Room, glancing side to side and behind me every now and then to make sure I wasn't being followed.

As I moved toward the sounds, I thought of a million reasons why I should about-face and go in the opposite direction. Didn't curiosity always kill that god-darn cat?

Once I reached the mouth of the hallway, I froze. Memories of the Safe Room rushed back and hit me like a bulldozer, the terrible images flickering in my mind.

I heard voices not too far off, intermixed with a steady, low buzzing. I had to see what it was. There were small, square windows on the hallway doors, about a foot wide and a foot long. If I was careful, I could peer inside and find out what was happening.

Creeping forward a few more feet, I arrived at the door where the sounds were coming from.

My heart raced. What if someone walked out right now and caught me sneaking around? I'd be in deep shit. Maybe they'd toss me into the Safe Room for a long stretch—a clinical lobotomy streamed directly into the cortex.

But I had to know.

I rose from my haunches toward the window.

What the—

I quickly crouched back down.

Batgirl was inside. She lay flat on her back, restrained on a gurney. A headset of some sort was clamped to her head, with wires snaking toward a computer tower. The machine, if I had to guess, was the source of that deep, low buzzing. Her eyes were rolled back—nothing but the whites showing—and she was shaking.

That woman, the director—what was her name? She was fiddling with a machine that looked like an EKG machine, but it must've been something completely different. Jack was there with her, assisting her.

Then it came to me—I remembered seeing a version of this in a TikTok video. It was electroshock therapy, and they were giving it to Batgirl. Her name is actually Christine. The poor thing looked like she was having a massive seizure. Her teeth were clattering together so hard I thought they might shatter.

White foam spilled from the corners of her mouth. My stomach lurched, and I fought the urge to throw up.

Dammit, I couldn't leave after seeing that. Even though Batgirl was admittedly pretty crazy, I couldn't let them do this to her. I had to find out what was happening. There was too much going on here, and I had to get to the bottom of it.

I snuck back the way I'd come and returned to my room. I figured it had been a good trial run for a real escape later on. I just couldn't leave one of my fellow girls high and dry—at the mercy of these creeps.

Luckily, no one spotted me. I slunk back into bed and thought about the plan I'd propose to Bex tomorrow. I had to convince her to escape with me. Maybe we could find a way to save Batgirl from electroshock therapy, and ferret her along. We'll hash out a plan tomorrow over breakfast, and I'm thinking we'll leave tomorrow night. They'll be the Anglin brothers to my Frank Morris—the other two inmates who escaped from Alcatraz. Something in my gut told me the staff here were doing terrible things to the girls—even worse than what they'd done to me, or anything I could imagine. I'd feel too guilty breaking out of this place and leaving them behind. I just had to come up with a plan. Fuck this place. I'm out.

Hey,

This isn't Sue. It's Bex.

Who the hell doesn't know what trans is? It's 2026. Has she been living under a goddamn rock? She must have never opened up Instagram, or ever watched much TV. Like ever. Her TikTok algorithm must be a stream of cute cats and dogs. I'm really at a loss.

Even so, I really do miss her. She was a cool cat. I'm also pretty worried about her disappearance. One theory I've been contemplating is that she may have gotten caught when she attempted to run away, and they're keeping her in solitary confinement somewhere.

Obviously, I didn't try to escape with her, otherwise I wouldn't be here right now, scribbling in her journal. She tried to coax me to leave with her on that fateful night in July. I told her she'd lost her marbles and she was going to get caught. Well, what do you know? It seems that's exactly what happened. Just because I was right doesn't mean I'm happy about it. I'm devastated that she's gone. I just hope she's okay —wherever she is.

I found her journal in the ceiling of the girls' bathroom when I was searching for a new place to hide my vape.

To whomever finds this journal—this place *is* completely fucked.

I just read through Sue's diary entries. Admittedly, it's a major breach of privacy, but here's the thing: Sue isn't here anymore. No one knows what happened to her. I last saw her on July 14th at dinner. I've asked her roommate and the counselors, and no one can give me any intel; no one can give me a straight answer.

I can't write for long. I have to be at meditation in about fifteen minutes.

So let me get right to it.

The Safe Room Sue was taken to is different from the one I was brought to. After reading about the room Batgirl was in, that's also completely different from my experience. I'd rather not write down what happened to me in there, I'm actively trying to forget it. Thinking about it gives me chills and makes me feel incredibly nauseous. Maybe once more time passes, I'll be able to talk about it or write about it here, but not right now.

Instead, I'll tell you a little about my story and how I ended up here.

Both my parents died in a gruesome car accident three years ago. My aunt, whom I love dearly, took me in and cared for me afterward. At least, she tried for a while. God bless her soul, but I was just too much of a rabble-rouser for her to handle. I think her heart was in the right place when she decided to send me to the Palisades Girls Academy. Unfortunately, parents and guardians have no idea just how evil this place is. They're fooled by the institute's catchy marketing, quaint façade, manicured landscaping, and fake smiles—all of which paint it as a therapeutic center.

Well, I have a theory. Not only are we being abused, both mentally and physically, I think these evil pricks are running experiments on us. After having read Sue's account, I think they're not only testing state-of-the-art mind-control interfaces, but they're also experimenting on us with all sorts of drugs—from painkillers, benzos, anti-manics—the whole gamut. It's like a modern day MKUltra, only done under the guise of a reformatory, or whatever the hell this place is called. If you're not familiar with what MKUltra is then you'll have to just look it up on your own time. They've definitely shot me up with some heavy-duty stuff. It's messed with my memory and also my nervous system. I feel different compared to how I felt when I first rolled in here. It's difficult to describe—I just feel weak. If

I've got the dates correct, I've been here for a little over two months.

All right. I've got to go. I'm going to hide the journal now. I'll be back and report when I can. And in keeping with Sue's valediction: Peace out.

Hey,

Bex here. I didn't have a chance to check in yesterday, so I'll have to fill you in on what's happened these last couple of days. Yesterday began just like every other ordinary day here at Palisades. I went to breakfast, then had counseling later in the morning. There's a new girl in our group. I'll refer to her as Bambi because she looks like a deer caught in headlights all day long. She looks completely lost, like she has no idea where she is or how she ended up here. Whoever dropped her off must've played a sick prank on her because judging by the look on her face, she's still coming to terms that she's not in Kansas anymore. And she's dead right. We're so many miles away from Kansas, it's not the slightest bit funny. We might as well be on the moon or some other planet. I had to corner her somewhere in private and interrogate her. She could be the key to me finding out some answers about this dreadful place.

I waited until lunchtime to approach her. She was sitting at a table by herself and still had that deer in the headlights look.

I sat down next to her and said, "Hey, Bambi."

She stared at me for a moment and replied, "That's not my name."

"I know, silly." I gave her a friendly smile, attempting to break the ice, which hopefully told her I meant her no harm. "I'm Bex. It's short for Rebecca."

"Nice to meet you." She lowered her head and continued munching on her tuna sandwich.

"So, why are you here?"

"That's personal and none of your business."

"Look, I get it. You don't know me from Adam, but you need allies here." I looked from left to right. Anytime I put my tinfoil hat on, I had to make sure there weren't any screws around. You can't be too careful around this place. "This place is completely fucked, Bambi."

She gave me a funny look like she actually saw the proverbial tinfoil hat resting on my head. She was probably thinking, *has this girl taken her meds today?* But the reality was she only just got here and doesn't have the slightest clue how frightening this place actually is. She's no idea about girls suddenly disappearing, the random room raids at three in the morning, the Safe Room. I was just trying to find any clues that would give me answers to these nagging questions.

"Listen," —I pressed— "I need to know why you're here. I'm trying to connect some dots, and you might be able to help."

She looked at me, rolled her eyes, and went back to her sandwich.

"Please, just tell me."

"What do you want to know?"

"Why you're here. Or why you *think* you're here?"

I already knew the answer before she told me. I just had to hear it from the horse's mouth.

"Same reason you're here," she said. "My parents think you can pray the gay away." She went back to consuming her sandwich. Her hunched shoulders were a sign she had already capitulated and there was nothing that could be done to combat her fate—or *our* fate for that matter. "That's what this place is, isn't it?" Now her eyes told me she was afraid of the answer I was certain to give her.

"Yeah. That's what this place is."

We were both silent for a while.

"You're not gonna eat," she asked me.

"I don't really have an appetite."

"Can I have your sandwich?"

"Sure." I passed her my tray.

She kept her head down and kept on eating. I felt sick to

my stomach. *How could you do this to me, Constance?* My aunt —the woman I loved, the one I thought would be my tether— maybe she was just another victim of the Academy's lies. I wanted to believe she was blinded by the stately veneer and the manicured grass. I wanted to give her the benefit of the doubt. Because the alternative was worse: that her heart was colder than ice, and she had knowingly signed the papers to have me frayed in this God-forsaken hole.

After lunch we were corralled to meditation. Today was different, though. We were split up and I was taken to a room. There was a lounge chair in the center and a nurse instructed me to lie down on it and wait until the doctor arrived.

I lay down and kicked my feet up on it. It was actually quite comfortable.

As I stared at the ceiling, my thoughts returned to Constance. I had calmed down a little since lunch but a surge of resentment shot through me like a jolt of electricity. How could she? I had to talk to her. When was the next time I'd be able to call? Today was… Shit, what day is it today? As I lay on the soft, plush chair, I had difficulty remembering what day it was. Wasn't I supposed to be in meditation? What was I doing here in this room? My thoughts were muddled.

The door opened and someone entered the room. I shielded my eyes from the fluorescents to get a better look at who'd come in. He was a small man with round glasses and wore a sport coat and a wide tie with an abstract expressionism design.

"Hello, Rebecca," he said. His voice was soft and soothing. "I'm Doctor Hintermeyer."

"You can call me Bex," I said, stifling a yawn. The lights in the room dimmed.

"Please, close your eyes."

"Yes."

"Let my words come to you. There's nothing you have to think about. That's right." He exhaled softly.

"As you're letting these words come to you, notice that body in the chair. You'd probably rather be some place other than in this room, such as Aruba, so be there. Enjoy being there—the warm water, the white sandy beach."

I was perfectly obsequious as he spoke, my head sinking into the plush chair until the leather felt like warm, soft, damp sand. I closed my eyes and let the room dissolve, the gray walls bled into a pink horizon, and the hum of the fluorescents and forced air became the rhythmic, percussive crash of tropical waves. I'd never been hypnotized until then. It felt so easy, so natural.

"Good… that's right."

A hand began caressing me on my thigh. I wanted to pluck it off me but I was on a sandy beach and the sun was shining.

"Allow yourself to go deeper and deeper."

I was rubbing sunblock all over my pale legs and on my butt.

"Some people imagine floating down a cloud…" the hand climbed higher and higher up my thigh until it reached the hollow between my thighs.

"That's good, Rebecca…" I heard the doctor say. Then, I didn't remember anything else.

PART TWO

CHAPTER
ONE

SILVAINE DAVIES LOOKED up toward the door. Did she see someone at the window? Perhaps she was beginning to hallucinate. She'd been awake for more than twenty hours. Moreover, she'd taken double her usual dosage of Adderall, which helped keep her going all night as she labored. So much work had to be done, and she would not allow herself a minute of leisure. The Program was humming along like a well-oiled machine.

"Jack, can you go check to see if someone is out there?" she said to her assistant. "I thought I saw someone hovering at the glass."

"Certainly."

The assistant turned from the computer and made his way toward the door.

Davies continued monitoring the girl on the exam table. *This one will be difficult to rectify,* she thought. Some of the girls were more stubborn and posed a greater challenge than others, but Davies welcomed challenges. It made her tenure at the Academy more illuminating.

"Hey!" Jack shouted. She heard the pounding of his footsteps echo down the corridor.

"Oh, what now?" Davies muttered. She checked the restraints to ensure they were latched securely, making certain the girl wouldn't be able to wander if she regained consciousness. Once satisfied, she crossed to the door and followed the sound of pounding feet.

When she'd reached Jack, he had already caught up with the escapee and was mounted on top of her. What a sight it was. The girl's long hair whipped wildly as she bucked and flailed, her back pinned to the floor. At first, Davies had difficulty identifying who she was. Jack was struggling to hold down her wrists. Poor chap was more spindly than she found ideal, but he was loyal and compliant and carried out his duties without grumbling. The young girl was admittedly putting up a good fight. She was a strong little bitch. *We'll see what happens after she's been here for a few more months*, Davies thought.

Two nurses had arrived already. Carmen held a syringe fully-loaded with Propofol, attempting to find an opening where she could go in and shoot the girl with it. Dwayne, the other nurse, held down the girl's legs so she wouldn't kick or knee. As Davies got a closer look, she recognized the escapee. Her name was Susan Colt, a relatively new admit who had arrived at Palisades only two weeks prior. Already, she'd found herself in a world of trouble. *Shame, shame, shame,* Davies thought.

There'd been only one other girl who had spied on their procedures being carried out in one of the Safe Rooms in the eighteen months since the program's inception. Admittedly, safeguards around the facility had slackened, the rationale aimed at presenting the girls with the *illusion* they were free. It was quite the contrary as they were constantly being monitored and surveilled. Davies thought of the last girl who had spied on their confidential procedures. Jane Castro. It took some maneuvering but they were able to make her disappear. She showed up to Palisades with a long history of being a runaway, so Silvaine and the two other board members were only questioned once by police. Most staff were unaware of what had happened. The clinical psychologist thought Jane had actually run away, as did most staff members. Jack—the counselor who was Davies's menial—and a couple of nurses, however, knew what had really happened to her. Davies had to pay them an astronomical amount of hush money to keep them quiet. The detectives ate up their tale, after which they informed the girl's foster parents that she had simply run away. Everyone believed The Palisades Academy was in the upper echelons of therapeutic boarding schools in the Northeast. The administration, including Silvaine Davies, was regarded with the utmost esteem, so no one, including law enforcement, probed any further.

Carmen had stuck the plunger into Susan's right arm. In just a few moments, her movements were already sluggish and the thrashing had subsided.

Davies stood over the girl, admiring her soft features. Susan was beautiful, and the Director had big plans for her. *She will be my new little project,* Davies thought, as a lurid smile spread across her face.

Dwayne pushed a gurney, and with Carmen's help, they hoisted and slid Susan onto it. She fell back and lay recumbent, in a comatose state.

"Take her to the service level," Davies told the nurses flatly. "Lock her in the cage."

Dwayne nodded, then pushed the girl toward the elevator.

Excitement grew inside the director. These were the perks —the fruits of labor claimed by those who occupy the throne.

"Hello?" Sue's voice echoed. She'd awakened on a cot two hours later in pitch-darkness. Her head was left feeling like it was splitting into two halves after the effects of the drug had worn off. Almost all light was extinguished, except for a lone utility bulb that shined a frail glow, radiating from a distance. Susan's eyes took a minute to adjust, until finally, she saw where they'd put her—a squalid cell. She felt around her perimeter, examining the nearby walls. Metal bars enclosed the opposite side of her cage. As she patted around, the rough cement felt like cinder blocks. She sat up on the cot, then stood carefully, shuddering as her bare feet touched the cold floor. With her fingertips, she mapped the geometry of her confinement.

Susan remembered the arrogant-looking, stone-faced woman. She'd seen her that time briefly in the cafeteria, and she was the one who'd been cooking Batgirl's brains with raw voltage. She must be the director—the head master—the one pulling all the strings. Sue thought back to her first day at the academy. During intake, her parents had met with the directors, but she had been sent to the psychologist. Odd she'd never really seen the woman around the facility besides that one time. *Nice going*, Mom and Dad, *handing me over to the antichrist*.

"Heeelloooooo?" she yelled. Fear began to bubble inside her. Trapped in a pall of total darkness, Sue admitted the unthinkable: she'd rather be back in her room with Chatterbox, listening to her endless drivel, than the crushing dark she presently found herself in.

She called out for another ten minutes, then stopped when her vocal cords began to feel raw and tender. No one came. She slunk back into the cot and clutched at her threadbare blanket, wondering how long she'd be punished for this time around.

The night was a stifling haze of drifting in and out of strange dreams, and struggling to find a comfortable position on the granite slab of a cot. In one dream, she found herself in a screaming match with her father, berating him for sending her to Palisades. In another, she was tossing dirt on her mother's casket. The cemetery was a phalanx of mourners, veiled faces in black weeping into tissues and handkerchiefs. Glancing up, she saw a dull gray sky opening above her. Father Donnelly, the priest from her parish, rebuked her for her transgressions. He waved his left hand admonishingly at her and hissed, "God shall scourge your flesh with eternal fire, girl! He has already damned your spirit to the stony depths of Hell!"

Sue woke to a sudden surge of white light. Her body ached as she rolled away, shielding her eyes from the painful glare. Days usually began punishingly early at the Academy, but this felt exceedingly so. A door clanged open, and the staccato click of heels signaled someone's rapid approach.

The stone-faced woman appeared under the fluorescents.

"Who are you?"

"We haven't had the pleasure of meeting yet, Susan. I've been a little tied up with administrative duties since your arrival." Her tone was all business. "I am Silvaine Davies, Director of the Academy."

"So, you're the bitch in charge of this place?"

"You can say that." Silvaine's eyes were latched on the girl. "But, may I remind you, foul language is not tolerated at the Palisades Academy for Young Women and Teens. You will be punished for cussing."

"Fuck you!" Sue barked back. She wondered what the director planned to do with her. If it weren't for the metal bars that separated the two of them, she would give the old cunt a taste of her wrath. "How long are you keeping me down here?"

"A few weeks, maybe a few months. I haven't really decided yet."

Sue scowled at her, then clutched the bars with white-knuckled rage. "You can't do that," she said, her voice oscillating with anger. "My parents won't allow it!" She stood nearly two feet from the woman and was breathing hard.

Sue didn't see what came next, as the woman snaked a cattle prod through a gap in the bars and electrocuted her for nearly ten interminable seconds. Her body thrashed and flailed uncontrollably like a Baptist laity. When Davies removed the prod from the girl's stomach, her legs folded and she collapsed backwards. The stench of charred flesh and searing skin saturated the cell as Sue lay clutching her gut in fierce pain.

"In time, you'll learn to be respectful," Davies said. She turned and clicked her heels down the corridor, leaving Sue gasping for air and crying in agony.

The skin on her stomach began to pucker and molt. The second she touched it, she yelped. The cattle prod had severely burned her.

"I'm gonna fucking kill you," Sue muttered in the darkness. It took her fifteen minutes to muster the energy to pick herself up off the ground and drag herself onto the cot.

She lay on her back, careful not to touch the wound. She removed her shirt and draped the blanket over her shoulders like a cape. Even the slightest touch of fabric—or the accidental brush of a finger against the burn—hurt as if raw flesh were being scrubbed with a Brillo pad.

Davies returned to her office, shutting the door behind her. She picked up the phone at her desk and dialed the Colt residence. Susan Colt's mother picked up on the third ring.

"Hello?"

"Hi, Mrs. Colt?"

"Yes, who's calling, please?"

"Hi, this is Silvaine Davies, Director of the Palisades Academy for Young Women."

"Oh, hi! How are you?" Mrs. Colt took a deep breath. "My husband and I have been trying to call the Academy, but keep getting an answering machine. I'm so glad you called. Is everything all right with Sue?"

"She has shown some emotional growth, but…"

"But—what is it?"

"Well, our doctor recommended a new medication for her, and I just wanted to run it by you and your husband first. We need you to give us the green light."

"What medication are they recommending?"

"As you know, Mrs. Colt, Dr. Hintermeyer, a Harvard University graduate and winner of several APA awards—"

"APA… what's that again?"

"The American Psychiatric Association," Davies replied flatly.

"Of course."

"He's a top-notch physician, Mrs. Colt," Davies continued. "I wouldn't want to steer you or your lovely daughter in the wrong direction. He recommended that we begin to give Susan Clozapine. It will help with her aggression." She paused. *Roll over, you damn bitch*, Davies thought. "She's been harming herself, and the doctor strongly recommends she take it. It's for her own safety."

"Oh, my God. Harming herself? How? Is she cutting?" The words were rushing out of her mouth and her alarm was palpable. "I thought that wasn't likely to happen there? Isn't she being monitored?"

"Yes, she is. But the patients find ways, Mrs. Colt. That's precisely why the doctor recommends the medication."

Davies heard her breathing into the telephone—heavy, exasperated breaths. She was accustomed to this type of resistance. Eventually, parents or guardians realized what had to be done for their delinquent children, and they ultimately caved.

"OK. Fine." Her tone was pitiable. "I'll speak with my

husband and update him. I hope the medication helps her. Poor thing."

"Wonderful," Davies said. "It will help. I've seen its positive effects first-hand with many other girls. We'll begin administering her with it as soon as it becomes available. Oh, and Mrs. Colt—"

"Yes?"

"When were you planning to visit Susan?"

"Hmm. Yeah. We were going to try to stop by next weekend and see her."

Davies groaned wearily into the receiver. "I don't think that would be a wise decision. Is there any way you could postpone your visit for at least a few weeks?"

"A few weeks?" she gasped. "Why should we wait so long to see her?"

"Well, there is an adjustment period for the medication. Susan is still in phase one of her recovery, so her frame of mind is still tenuous. She may be all out of sorts for a little while. How about you reschedule for next month so you have a better experience when you see her again?"

"Next month?" the mother asked incredulously. "But—"

"I just don't want you or your husband to be unsettled when you see her."

There was a long pause. *Just say yes, you dumb bitch. We're the experts here. You're nothing but a simpleton.*

"Christ, is it *that* bad?"

"It won't be in a few weeks, which is why you and Mr. Colt need to trust us—you need to have some faith in our clinical team. We know what we're doing. I've been doing this for over twenty years and, as you're well aware, our academy has won many accolades. We have the most talented doctors and staff in our employ. Please, trust our expertise."

Davies did not have to press further. Mrs. Colt agreed her and her husband would refrain from visiting the academy for at least a few weeks, or at least until Sue had adapted to her new medications. The director smiled bitterly as she glanced at her computer screen. On the monitor, Susan shuddered under her blanket. It was a private video feed, accessible only to Davies. The pain the young girl was experiencing must be profound, she reflected, having prodded her with high voltage for several seconds.

The director pressed a button, and a moment later, the cell went dark. Davies stared at the monitor, fantasizing about the acts she had planned for Susan Colt. Her lurid thoughts made her ache with desire. She would have her, Davies thought. She would have her soon.

SILVAINE DAVIES, Director of the Palisades Academy for Young Women, entered the boardroom. She was greeted by expressionless men in black tailoring and crisp, laundered shirts, their ties knotted with tight precision. She'd been dreading the meeting since she was first notified about it a few days prior. Something about an audit from the state happening in a week. Apparently the state doesn't give much notice when it decides to kick the tires and comb through the books. If it were any other time, it'd be hardly a challenge for her and her team. But her mind gravitated to Susan Colt, who was currently being held in a subterranean cell. She hadn't quite figured out how she was going to deal with that loose thread, but she and her team at the Academy had to come up with a plan, and it had to be done quickly.

Davies saw an unoccupied chair at the conference table and sat, joining the group.

"Thank you for coming on such short notice, Silvaine," Bill Dunkle, the CFO of the organization, said. "When it comes to these matters—matters involving the state—all our ducks need to be in a row. We can't give those bastards any room to come after us."

"Of course, William. We're a fairly new treatment center, so it was only a matter of time before they paid us a visit," she replied.

Davies felt every eye in the room on her and sensed their critical scrutiny.

"How are things going at the Academy?" Albert Weer asked. Weer was the CEO and founder of the Palisades Academy for Young Women and several other teen residential treatment centers across the country. He'd been on-site almost daily for the first three months to ensure things were operational, but he was completely hands-off now. With his attention consumed by a multitude of other startups and charities, Davies saw him only a few times a year, mostly at board meetings or endowment galas. He only cared about two things: that the investment stayed in the black and that there were no fires to put out. Davies intended to give him exactly what he wanted.

"Business is running as smoothly as ever at the farm," she replied.

One of the lead psychologists frowned at her. She meant the *funny farm*. On other occasions, she'd refer to Palisades as *The Bin*—a cynical nod to the antiquated term *loony bin* (of course she would only speak like this in private, and never at the Academy). Her dark humor was not appreciated by everyone present, least of all the mental health professionals. Several grumbled under their breath at her uncouth remark.

She took a deep breath and rolled her shoulders back until her shoulder blades pressed together. Her breasts tightened the fabric across her chest. She could sense the men drooling, gazing at her assets. Davies was admittedly not the most attractive woman in the world—not that she was unattractive —but in the context of this sausage fest, these dogs wouldn't hesitate to pounce on the opportunity to take a turn with her.

Martin, the Vice President of operations, practically had his tongue lolling on the table.

"Very well," Weer replied. He then turned to Dunkle, the *money* guy, and asked him about the Academy's financials. Dunkle sifted through the pages of numbers and charts in front of him, at which point Davies had tuned out. To her, it was tedious drivel, a distraction from her real work. She figured the Academy was doing well financially since residential and clinical fees were exorbitant and enrollment was at maximum capacity.

Davies began to fantasize about Susan. She wanted her isolated, without supervision from the therapists and counselors, and the cameras turned off. Then, she'd really test the little misfit. She'd show that bitch who was boss, Davies thought. She was practically trembling with excitement at the thought of it.

"Silvaine… Hey, Silvaine… you okay?" Dunkle had been calling her.

"Yes, I'm sorry." She snapped back to the conference room. "What were you saying?"

"We were commending you," Weer cut in, "on all the excellent work you and your team have been doing at the Academy. Profits are soaring and we are planning to open a new facility toward the end of next year. Keep doing what you're doing, Silvaine."

"I'm glad you're happy with my performance. If it weren't for my exceptional team, we wouldn't be here right now, seeing all this operational success."

During the remainder of the meeting, the suits coached Davies on what to say and what information to withhold during the state's visit. Many of them would be present on that day to support her, including Andrew Weer. Having Weer there with her made her feel more at ease. He was a keystone when it came to shaking hands with stiff, pedantic bureaucrats. The man could sell climate change to a Republican. All that was well and good, and Silvaine had no issues handling bureaucrats of all types and levels, herself, but one complication continued to nag her. What the fuck was she going to do with Susan while they were there, poking their heads around, inspecting the facility?

~

My parents are going to visit me at some point, Susan Colt thought. *That sociopath can't keep me down here forever.* She glanced around her cell. The facility's underbelly gave her the creeps. There were no windows. They'd left the lights on for her, but there wasn't much to see. Beyond the cell there was the lengthy corridor that led to a door that the staff used to come in and out of. The walls were raw cement. Sue looked up at the ceiling. Rusted pipes hissed and clicked incessantly throughout the day and night, disturbing her sleep when she dozed off.

She had to go to the bathroom. She'd been holding it in for over an hour now. At first Sue thought they would take her back upstairs to use the facilities, but that didn't seem to be a part of their plan. There was no toilet in the cell. Instead, they'd left a metal bucket in the corner, and after hours of isolation, the sinking reality of its purpose finally dawned on her.

Her stomach was hurting and she wasn't sure how much longer she could hold out. She paced around the cell, biding her time, but she was going to burst any second. *God help me.*

The bucket was calling her name. What other option did she have? She raced over to it and positioned it as far away from her cot as she could, then squatted and let her bowels loose. After about thirty seconds of squatting, her thighs began to burn. She was afraid to look down to assess her accuracy, knowing her aim hadn't been completely flawless. Once she felt like she had completed the act and could stand back up, dread began to set in. What was she going to use to wipe herself with? There was nothing in her bare cell besides her flimsy blanket. She made a last-minute decision, used her sweatpants to wipe, and stuffed them into the bucket. They're going to have to give me new bottoms now, she figured, as she pushed them in to cover her waste. Once she was through, she left the bucket near the edge of the cell, far away from her cot so she wouldn't have to endure the smell.

She returned to her cot and huddled under her blanket, attempting to find warmth. Feeling less than clean and now naked from the waist down, Sue began to cry. She begged God, hoping someone would come to remove the bucket and give her a pair of sweats. The hours elapsed, and no one came to bestow upon her the dignity of a sanitized environment.

CHAPTER
THREE

REBECCA "BEX" Simon spotted Christine Peters, aka Batgirl, in the cafeteria and sat down right next to her.

"Sup, slut."

"Hey, Bex."

"Listen, I can't stop thinking about Sue since the night she disappeared."

"Nice to see you, too, bitch."

"Yeah, yeah, yeah." Bex could sense the other girl's annoyance—the realization that she was only being spoken to because Bex wanted something. She wasn't wrong. Regardless, Bex needed answers. There was a nagging feeling in her gut telling her Sue could be in trouble. "Aren't you worried? What do you remember about the last night we all saw her? Do you remember anything that might give me a clue?"

Christine rolled her eyes and sighed. "Dumb girly, Sue went home."

Bex narrowed her eyes at her. "What's wrong with you? Open your goddamn fucking eyes. Can't you see this place is completely fucked!" She let the words fly a little too loud. A counselor standing ten feet away heard her and made his way over. "Shit…"

"Now look what you've done."

A counselor Bex didn't recognize—probably in his twenties and fresh out of college—approached her. The Academy seemed to have a revolving door when it came to staff. They were overworked, short-staffed, and the pay was likely crap.

"Rebecca Simon…"

"Yeah?"

"You know the policy. This is your first warning today. Curse again and you'll be put in the Safe Room."

"I'm sorry. I won't let it happen again." Bex's insides got all shivery at the mention of that god-forsaken room. She'd rather lick the counselor's toes than get sent back there and experience that hell again.

He turned and walked away, leaving her with a warning.

Bex was frustrated that Christine was so clueless about their friend's sudden disappearance. Why would her parents pick her up in the middle of the night? The counselors and staff—all culpable parties—swore she'd been discharged, that her parents had picked her up and taken her from the Academy. But that didn't line up. If she had been taken out, it likely would have happened in the morning or afternoon, not in the middle of the night.

The key piece of information came from Chatterbox earlier that day. According to the horse's mouth, she'd seen Sue in their room on the evening of July 14th. Bex had already tried prying as much information as she could from the girl, but she—that goddamn girl—should have been a politician. She had a mouth on her (not in that way), but it was impossible to keep her on one topic for more than a few seconds. She'd circumvent questions with tangential nonsense. Bex had tried to probe her several times and grew so impatient she thought she would end up strangling the stupid lump.

So, Christine was her next hope. Bex had a plan, she just had to convince her. She cracked her knuckles and got right in Christine's face.

"Listen," Bex whispered, leaning in closer to ensure no one heard their conversation, and most importantly, no one heard her conspiracies. "I think Sue's still here… somewhere."

"They've really scrambled your brains, haven't they?" Christine said, cackling wildly.

Bex put a hand over the girl's mouth. "Keep it down, will you," she snapped. "I already got a warning."

Luckily the counselor who'd warned her was presently on the far end of the cafeteria and there were no other staff nearby.

"So, tell me, Sherlock, why do you think Sue's still here?"

"Don't you think it's weird she would just leave without saying goodbye to any of us?" Bex gestured toward Chatterbox. "And not even tell her roommate? It doesn't raise any alarm bells?"

"Nope. Not weird at all. I've been here for three months and have already seen several girls come and go, most without a single *adios, arrividerci, au revoir…* nada, you get me?"

"Sue's different. She's our homegirl. Something inside me tells me she never went home. Are you that naive about this place?"

Christine gave her a stern look. "It's not that I'm naive. I know this place is fucked—" she checked around to ensure no one was eavesdropping. "—It's just that I don't want to go back to that fucking room."

She had a point. It'd been weeks since Bex had been sent to the Safe Room. She didn't remember much from that last stretch. They'd given her heavy-duty sedatives, and the experience had been nothing more than a vague delirium. She didn't know what was more frightening—the spotty recollection of being dragged to a white-tiled room and injected with a tranquilizer that put her out almost immediately, or the lack of any memory regarding the horrors they must have subjected her to.

"I don't want to go back either," Bex replied.

"Meet me in the bathroom after lunch," Christine suggested. We'll have some time to kill before meditation. I'll tell you what I know." She glanced over at the counselors who stood, watching the patients closely. "They won't be able to hear us with the shower running."

"Good idea. I'll meet you there."

Half an hour later, Bex had undressed in her room and slipped into her robe. With her towel and her bag of toiletries in hand, she made her way to the third-floor bathroom. She placed her belongings on the vanity then looked at herself in the mirror. There were puffy bags underneath her eyes. She never looked this wasted, she thought. She'd been shedding pounds during her internment. It seemed everyone she talked to agreed the food was getting worse and worse, so the solution was not to eat it. Her nerves were as brittle as dried out flowers. The Palisades Academy for Young Women and Teens was the opposite of therapeutic. They were slowly killing her in that hell-hole, everything from the spur-of-the-moment room checks at dawn, to the meditation sessions, which were nothing more than emotional bullbaiting sessions. They were slowly chipping away at her.

Bex stepped into the shower and turned on the water. The water that came out was freezing. She leaped out of the stream, waited thirty seconds, then checked the temperature. It was warming up. In another minute, the shower poured onto her and began to steam into the bathroom.

She heard the door open. Someone had entered.

"Bex, you in here?" It was Christine, just outside the curtain.

"I'm in the shower." Bex had her eyes shut. She was massaging her hair with shampoo and lathered her body with soap, working it into her shoulders and then her legs. The hot water felt so good as it sluiced all over her.

Then suddenly, Bex yelped and sprang backwards in the shower.

"What the fuck?" A hand had touched her. She opened her eyes, fighting through the stinging soap. "What the hell are you doing?"

Christine stood in the shower, naked, just a foot away from her.

"What do you want to know?"

"You have to get out of here! Now! We'll get in so much trouble."

Christine reached out and caressed Bex's breasts. She pulled her in close and forced her tongue in her mouth. Bex moaned softly as the water splashed on their heads, acquiescing in her friend's grasp.

Bex felt a hand touch down below and then delicate fingers probed her slit. Her back pressed against the shower wall. In between gasps and moans, Bex took hold of Christine's finger and slid it into her wet warmth. Pulsing ecstasy filled her sensory hotspots.

They froze when the bathroom door suddenly opened and someone walked in.

"Rebecca, are you in here?"

Jesus! It was one of the female counselors.

Bex was breathing hard. Christine put her hand up to her lips and mouthed *shhhhh…* and then *breathe.* She took a few quick breaths, relaxed, and then replied, "Yes, I'm taking a shower."

"Hurry up, will you. Meditation's in ten minutes and you have to be present. Don't be late."

"Okay, I'm almost done. I won't be late."

They heard the door close. Christine started laughing, which made Bex nervous. If they were to get caught in the shower together, who knows what kind of punishment they'd decide on for the both of them.

"Listen, we'll talk another time, but I don't think you should bother looking for Sue." Christine knew something had happened to Sue, she was just too afraid to dig into the matter. It gave Bex more conviction that her hunch held weight. She'd press her another time. She also decided she'd have to circle back and try to pry some more information out of Chatterbox, though she dreaded the encounter.

Christine kissed Bex and whispered, "To be continued," before slipping out of the shower.

BEX WAITED until the next day when they were allotted an hour to congregate in the yard before approaching Chatterbox. She remembered when she'd gotten to the Academy, there were hiking trails nearby. One in particular was within walking distance of the facility, but its entrance was gained from the front of the building. Out here in the back, besides the expansive lawn and the track, she'd forgotten all about the nature walks that the facility used as a selling point to entice unsuspecting parents with fat wallets who could foot the bill. She wouldn't dare ask about it. She'd been punished enough in the three months she'd been there, and had learned to conform, at least in the eyes of the screws.

Chatterbox was talking to a newer admit at the table when Bex approached them and butted right in their conversation. "Hey, new girl, can you give me and Motormouth some privacy. I need to speak with her."

The new girl looked up at Bex, scowling. She clenched her fists and began to stand up.

Chatterbox put out a hand to calm her down. "Chill, Andrea. This is Bex. We're cool."

"Bitch don't look cool," the new girl replied.

"I have some important things I need to talk to her about, and it doesn't involve you. Don't take it personally." Bex's tone was placid. She was not a fighter and had no desire to get wrapped up in any physical altercations.

Andrea stood up and got in Bex's face. Chatterbox pulled her away.

"Listen, you have no idea what they'll do to you if you throw a punch," Chatterbox said. "Trust me, okay?"

The new girl glared for a moment then seemed to loosen up, relaxing her stance. "Yeah, whatever," she replied, then turned and left them.

"What's this about?" Chatterbox asked.

"Let's walk." Bex led her toward the track where they would be able to talk more freely without the risk of being overheard. Once they were fifty yards away from the nearest counselor, she said, "It's about Sue. What do you remember about the last night you saw her."

"It was sometime in July."

"July 14th to be exact," Bex said.

"That's right. We went to bed that night just like we did every other night. The lights went off, and we fell asleep."

"So, when did they summon Sue? The story they told us is her parents came and picked her up, and she was discharged, right? I'm trying to figure out when she actually left."

"I haven't a clue, Bex. I woke up and she was gone. I guess they must've grabbed her in the middle of the night."

"You don't think that's a little strange? That her parents would show up to take her out in the middle of the night." Bex shook her head, wishing Chatterbox could see her point. "It just doesn't add up."

"I guess it is kinda weird, now that you mention it."

They made two more laps around the track. Chatterbox went on a diatribe about her counseling session earlier that morning that Bex simply tuned out. While rounding the curve, Bex became self-conscious, and noticed some of the counselors had their eyes fixed on them. She then looked up at a second-floor window at the far end of the building. A glacial chill spread up her back. A vague figure seemed to be staring out at her. The figure was too far away for Bex to capture any details, but whoever it was seemed to be watching them closely.

They returned to the cohort where the other girls were idling about sitting at tables, gabbling inanities.

"If you think of or remember anything else, just let me know, will you?"

"Sure thing, Sherlock." Before Chatterbox turned to go back inside the building, she moved in close and asked very quietly, "What do *you* think happened to her?"

Bex whispered, "I think she's still here… somewhere."

Chatterbox's eyes opened wide and for the first time since their interaction, Bex thought she was finally understanding. "Are you serious?"

"It's a very real possibility."

Chatterbox muttered, "Shit," before both girls walked back inside.

Bex was dreading going back in. She'd just started phase two of her treatment program, and things began to get even weirder at the Palisades Girls Academy for Young Women and Teens.

CHAPTER
FIVE

CHRISTINE PETERS, whom Sue referred to as Batgirl in jest, sat up from the couch in the TV room and meandered to her quarters. Her roommate, Julie, was already in bed, sulking in the dark, hating herself, as was usually the case with the depressed girl. Christine didn't talk to her much. She preferred to keep her distance. Every interaction she had with her roommate was negative. Julie had an incredibly dismal disposition and never had anything positive or uplifting to say. Even just being near her, Christine felt her melancholy seemed to drain her energy. Apparently she'd tried to kill herself more than a dozen times. And her parents believed Palisades was going to cure her, or fix her. If the poor bastards only knew.

Is it really that hard to kill yourself, anyway? Christine thought. Just get a hold of a gun, stick the barrel right in your mouth, and *BAM*. Julie had opened up to her early on when they were first introduced to each other, and what she told Christine had been really unsettling. Christine, admittedly, had her issues, but *man*, Julie was warped. One time the lunatic turned on her dad's car in the garage and attached a hose to the exhaust, and huffed carbon monoxide for half an hour. Luckily, her dad had gotten home just in time to find her and drag her out before she'd ended it.

The most gruesome story Julie had shared with her roommate was her first attempt ever at ending her life. It happened while she was in the ninth grade at the Catholic school she'd been attending. Julie had to wear a dress shirt and pleated skirt every day, along with high stockings. Nothing flattering. Christine imagined her looking like a goddamn nun. They may have just made her wear a scapular with a veil, and locked a chastity belt around her small ass. Christine loathed religion, especially Catholicism. She'd been raised in a Lutheran household and thank God (no pun intended), her parents weren't the church-going types. But she hated the Catholics because they hated her. They despised her for the simple reason that she was gay. Well, she wasn't fully gay. She liked boys, too. *Sometimes.* If she were to take a sexual preference test, she'd circle *all of the above.* Ever since she learned that hypocritical detail about the church, she never took organized religion, especially Christianity seriously. So, she felt sympathy for Julie, who was forced to go through all that jazz.

It happened during the school day, just before lunch. She'd been given a small box of tools for her biology lab. The toolkit included scalpels, scissors, tweezers, probes, needles—the whole gamut. Apparently Julie had removed the scalpel from the kit and locked herself in a stall in the girls' bathroom and carved deep, geometric slices into her wrists. A girl from her grade knocked on the stall door when she heard someone's bulk slam into the partition. Hearing no response from the occupant whose blood began to pool across the tile floor like a scarlet river, the girl decided to bang on the door, and force it open. She got it open with a forceful kick. What she found was poor little Julie, wedged in between the toilet and the partition, the skin on her wrists flayed in horrific patterns, exposing ribbons of tendons. The blood created a small lake on the bathroom floor in minutes. The horrified girl's scream was heard by Sister Mary Margaret, who then raced over from her classroom, just in time to find Julie before the unconscious girl met Saint Peter on the red carpet. They called 911 and an ambulance arrived in minutes. Julie was saved, and from the sound of it, it was nothing short of a miracle.

And that explained a lot of why her roommate was the way she was, Christine thought, as she slunk into bed. "Goodnight, Julie."

"Goodnight, slut." It was meant to be endearing, but lately it'd been bothering her more and more that some of the girls referred to her regularly with coarse monikers. It was either, *slut*, or *whore*, or *huzz*, and a few others Christine didn't care to remember, but she knew what they meant. The names had begun to lose their novelty, and were chipping away at her self-esteem.

"Can you get the light?" Julie asked.

Christine groaned. "Ugh, yeah," crawling back out of bed and going over to hit the switch. When she got to the door, she noticed Jack was staring in at her through the window. His presence startled her. They locked eyes for a few seconds. His waxen smile in the dim glow of the hallway gave her a creepy crawly feeling in her stomach. It was the same look, she thought, her old neighbor had given her just before he took her flower when she was nine years old. She tried to ignore it and returned back to bed. She was exhausted to her bones from the non-stop, nonsensical activities she'd participated in at Palisades. It was a day filled with meditation sessions that felt more like psychological torture, and she wondered how much more of the program she had to endure before she could return to her old life.

Christine was restless throughout the night. Tossing and turning in bed, her mind was flooded with dark dreams and nightmares. She'd tried to forget how they'd attached electrodes to her head and shocked her on several occasions.

They'd dulled her senses with anesthesia (she didn't feel a thing), and possibly a muscle relaxer, because she could hardly move when they racked her. God, how many times had they done it to her? Three, four times? It was all so foggy. The nurses inundated her and the other patients with so many pills that her memory had eroded.

She held the feeling of having to go to the bathroom for half an hour until her bladder could no longer take it. Rubbing the sleep from her eyes, she made her way to the restroom. It felt so nice to pee, she thought. There was no way she would've been able to hold it until morning. As she went to the bathroom, an image of Sue popped into her mind. Was it from her dreams earlier? Sue was trying to say something to her through the window, but she couldn't hear her. Christine tried to read her lips. Sue banged both her hands on the window with closed fists, looking distraught. Her hair, soaked from a bath or shower, whipped wildly. She was screaming now, looking like she was calling for help. Her eyes were red and puffy like she'd been crying for a while. *Help me!* she seemed to be saying. *Help me!* It was a portent. Christine was sometimes able to *see* the future or know when something bad was going to happen. She wasn't crazy or anything. It was something real. An early memory of a portent she experienced happened when she and her younger brother were playing in their driveway of their childhood home when she was seven years old. They were kicking their soccer ball back and forth when Christine had gotten a very strong, vivid image of her younger brother running into the street to retrieve the ball, only to get struck by a speeding car seconds later. The vision, which was the best way she could describe it, made her feel dizzy and weak, but when the soccer ball had slipped past her and her brother bolted into the street to get it, she lunged and tackled him. As soon as they were both on the ground, a large SUV sped down the blacktop at over fifty miles per hour.

This time, the vision of Sue made her reconsider her conversation with Bex. She knew she had to speak with her as soon as possible and figure out what it could mean. Maybe Sue was still at the Academy. Somewhere.

Christine flushed the toilet and exited the stall. Lost in her thoughts of Sue and her childhood memories, she nearly jumped out of her skin. Someone was there. Waiting.

CHAPTER
SIX

"HI, CHRISTINE."

It was Jack the counselor.

"Hi… um, what are you doing in the girls' bathroom?" There was an unsteady tremor that had slipped into her voice. "You're not supposed to be in here."

"You're not gonna tell on me, are you?"

She didn't like the way he was staring at her. It gave her a sudden rush of goosebumps and made her feel nauseous. "Please, get out. You're not supposed to be in the girls' bathroom."

"I can go wherever I please. I'm staff, and if I see it's necessary to enter the girls' bathroom, there's no rule or law that says I can't." He was smiling like a clinician who'd lost his mind.

He blocked the door. Christine weighed her chances of escape, but he had her trapped. Her heart raced. As he took several quick strides toward her, she turned and bolted into a stall, locking the door behind her.

"You can run but you can't hide," he jeered.

Shit. Christine felt like her heart was going to burst through her chest. She climbed onto the toilet and contorted into a protective crouch, watching the gaps below and the open space above.

A hand reached over the top of the stall and seized her. She screamed. Latching onto his wrist, she bit down on his hand with all her force.

"Ahhhhhh, you fucking little whore!"

Then she lunged out of the stall, crashing through the door and making a break for the exit. When she got there, she couldn't get it open. He'd locked it. *Dammit!* She spun around only to be stuck with a needle, and then she was struck violently across the jaw. The blow sent her tumbling into the tile wall, her head slamming against the hard surface.

Jack staggered toward her rubbing his injured hand. "That fucking hurt, you know that?"

Christine tried to pry herself up off the ground, groaning, dragging herself across the floor like a snail. The effects of the drug were beginning to dig their talons into her system, and her strength was waning fast.

"Don't worry, I didn't give you too much. Just enough so you'd be pliant, but not so much as to make you go unconscious. Cause fucking a girl who's passed out isn't fun."

"Ffffuck you!" Her words sounded slurred like she was drunk.

"You don't have to tell me twice," he said, removing his belt and pants.

Christine groveled on the floor, reaching for something to use as leverage, but the drug had done its job; her movements were in slow motion. He removed her sneakers, then her sweats, and finally her top.

He moaned as he caressed her breasts. "Yeah… oh, yeah." He took her limp hand and pressed it to his cock. She wanted to form a fist and punch him, but all her power had left her. She closed her eyes and wept as he entered her. He'd left her panties on, merely sliding them to the side. She envisioned all the ways she would inflict revenge on him when given the opportunity. That was all she could do as the vile pig forced himself on her while she lay in a catatonic state. The motherfucker would pay. He'd pay.

∼

Christine woke in her bed several hours later, the sheets drenched in sweat. She was afraid to move, the memory of the brutal assault from earlier that evening still raw. As she climbed down from the bunk, her legs felt unsteady and her body shook. She saw her roommate, Julie, lying in bed with her eyes wide open.

"Julie…"

"Are you okay?"

"Uh… I guess." She didn't want to get into it with her roommate, but her head felt heavy and her mind was clouded. The sedative she'd been given must have been incredibly potent. She almost slipped climbing down from the bunk.

"When they dragged you back in… you looked so out of it. What happened?"

"I don't remember." There was no way in hell she was going to talk about what had happened. She felt disgusting. *Violated* was too innocent of a word to describe what had been done to her. *Ravaged* was closer to the truth.

"God, Christine. This place gives me the willies."

Christine snickered. "What are you, a time traveler from the 1950s? Who the fuck says *'gives me the willies'*? She went to the closet, pulled out a towel, and patted herself dry.

"I grew up with my grandpa. I guess I picked up a lot of his slang."

Christine shook her head. "Keep talking like that, some of the girls here might give you a shiner…"

"A what?"

Christine rolled her eyes and said, "Just go to sleep, okay?"

"Okay… have a goodnight."

As Christine climbed back up to her bunk, she felt bad for talking to Julie like that. "Julie, I'm sorry I'm mean sometimes. This place—"

"It's okay. Don't worry about it. I know how this place can mess with your head."

"Yeah…" she said, as she laid the towel between her damp sheet and her back. Christine closed her eyes. Still feeling sore and aching, there was no way she'd get much rest. Not after what had happened. Her mind raced like a firing piston. She'd get revenge on the cocksucker, she was sure of it. The question of how she'd carry it out was a moot point. The real question was *when* she'd catch him.

CHAPTER
SEVEN

THE NEXT DAY AT LUNCH, Christine sought out Bex. She *had* to talk to her about the portent she'd had the night before.

Bex was sitting with Abby, whom Sue referred to as Helen Keller. She was a mousy girl, so soft-spoken that you had to ask "What?" five times before you heard a word she said. She also claimed she heard voices—which might have been factual—but Bex suspected Abby was putting on a ruse so the other girls wouldn't mess with her. If that were the case, Bex had to give the girl credit for her ingenuity. Usually, no one provoked someone who was too far gone. Any girl who was "cuckoo for Cocoa Puffs" was left alone, and Abby was one such girl.

No one really messed with Bex besides some of the counselors and security. At seventeen, she was one of the older girls in the program and saw herself as a mother hen for the younger patients. With only a few months left until she turned eighteen, Bex was counting down the days to freedom. But before she left the forsaken building, she had to find Sue. Even though she'd only known Sue for a brief period, she felt a bond with her—one she hadn't experienced even with her own siblings.

When Christine sat down next to her, Bex said, "Man, you look like shit. What happened to you?"

"Yeah… thanks. I'd rather not get into it."

"You know you can trust me, right? Didn't sleep last night? Let me guess—"

Christine cut in. "I wasn't taken to the Safe Room, if that's what you're going to say."

"Hmm... if it wasn't the Safe Room, then I'm not sure what else it could be. Unless—" Bex shot her a mischievous smile.

"I don't want to talk about it!" Christine snapped.

"Okay, okay, jeez. What the hell crawled up your ass?"

Christine dropped her head to the table and started sobbing.

"Ah, shit. I'm sorry, Chrissy," Bex said, rubbing her back. "I'm not sure what happened or what you're going through, but I'm really sorry."

She raised her head and dried her eyes. One of the female counselors made her way over and checked in to see what was happening.

"Are you okay, Christine?"

"Yeah, I'm fine." She had to compose herself. If they pulled her in this state, they'd question her for hours, and that was the last thing she wanted to deal with at the moment.

"Are you sure?" The counselor pressed. "Do you need to talk to someone?"

God, these counselors are relentless. All they want to do is mindfuck you, she thought. "Yes, I'm sure I'm fine," she said as evenly and calmly as she could manage, but her mind was screaming *LEAVE ME THE FUCK ALONE!* She had to bite her lip and refrain from telling her to get the fuck out of her face. Christine was well aware of what would happen if she antagonized the staff or exhibited even an iota of insubordination.

The screws loathed cursing. If the Code of Hammurabi were an allowable practice at Palisades, they'd chop an ear off for the girls' smallest transgressions. It never ended well for anyone who exhibited noncompliant behavior.

"You know you can talk to me, right?" Bex asked.

Christine glanced up at her. When she'd first arrived at Palisades, Bex had her hair short in a pixie-style cut. It had grown out since then. At Palisades, the girls were not allowed to style their hair or change it too drastically. Apparently, they did receive trims—at least, that's what Christine had once been told—but they hadn't cut hers yet. Or Bex's, for that matter, and she'd been there for five months already.

The cafeteria suddenly went silent. Christine followed Bex's eyes to the entryway, where Silvaine Davies, the director of the Palisades Academy for Young Women, marched in with a small platoon of functionaries. The suits trailed behind her like legionnaires. Davies's heels clicked against the floor. Today she must've been wearing four-inch heels, elevating her to an intimidating stature. The woman gave the impression she studied tape of the Third Reich; she strode with her chin pointed up, looking as if she were ready to snap a salute and yell *Sieg Heil!* Girls whispered, and the sounds of chewing and shuffling utensils drifted across the room. When Davies reached the center of the cafeteria, you could have heard a pin drop.

Everyone stared at the grim-faced woman. Those sitting closest to her swallowed. Even the hard girls at the Academy were humbled when Davies was around. Her presence alone was a force to be reckoned with. The woman was pure power.

Then, someone farted loudly. The cafeteria roared with laughter.

She yelled into the microphone. "QUIET!"

The laughter continued for a few seconds.

"I SAID QUIET!"

The giggling and whispers died instantly.

"For those of you who are new to Palisades, I'd like to welcome you," she continued. "In case you don't know who I am, my name is Silvaine Davies. I am the director of the Palisades Academy for Young Women and Teens." She rotated in a measured semicircle, her attention a monolithic force upon the room. "You are all incredibly lucky to be here, afforded the luxury and the privilege of being treated in such a marvelous institution with the best doctors and staff." Davies waved a hand toward her staff and the functionaries in suits. A few of them nodded in acknowledgment. "If you follow the steps toward recovery, you will be cured. Other girls have worked through the program, and they, too, were eventually reformed."

"Now," she barked into the microphone. "I have to turn to some important matters. We have a visit tomorrow from the state. They will be touring the academy, and we ask that you be on your best behavior. If any of them decide to speak with you, perhaps in passing, greet them politely. You should not only be on your best behavior, but we also expect you to show off your polished manners if the opportunity presents itself." She paused and glanced around the room. All eyes were glued to the woman. "Does anyone have any questions?"

Some dolt raised her hand. Davies rolled her eyes. "Yes?"

"Will all activities remain the same tomorrow? Can we still go to the yard for free time after lunch?"

"Yes, all activities will resume as scheduled. If you see us, or any staff, with someone you don't recognize, just assume they are with the state. And act accordingly. No shenanigans tomorrow. Are we all clear?"

No one responded.

"I said, are we all clear?" Davies screeched.

"Yes," the girls replied sonorously.

"Wonderful," she said. "Thank you for your time." She flashed a smile, then her lips returned to the straight, phlegmatic line that was their natural position. Davies turned and her heels clicked as she walked away, her functionaries trailing behind her like loyal vassals.

Christine whispered to Bex, "Sheesh, wouldn't want to be on that psycho's shitlist."

"She's an awful human being. Rumor is she drives a three hundred thousand dollar car."

"You're kidding me?" Christine said incredulously. "How do you know that?"

"Word gets around pretty quickly here. You know that."

"What kind of car is it?"

"A Bentley."

"Fuck. Bitch would drive a Bentley."

Christine felt the urge to tell Bex about what had happened to her the night before. She could trust her friend. But what good would it do? Bex might get furious and do something dumb, like attack Jack and then who knows what would happen to her. No, she decided she wouldn't tell her. She'd keep it to herself; it would be her little secret, just between her and Jack. The fucker would pay one day. For now, she'd share the portent she'd had about Sue. Maybe Bex was onto something regarding Susan Colt, and together they could figure out the mystery.

Sue sat hunched on the cot, clutching her stomach. She'd barely slept all night. The pain in her gut was ravaging, like sharp glass grinding at her midsection. A large, pus-filled bubble had formed. The sac of fluid was a bilious green that had been expanding for days, ever since Davies had struck her with the cattle prod. Now the pustule hurt like hell—a vast, searing pain she'd never experienced until now.

Sweat ran down her head and back. The sublevel had a cold, clammy feel. The industrial machines that inhabited the dark basement—the murmuring HVAC system, the buzzing electrical switchgear—never turned off, and they were starting to mess with Sue's mind. She thought she'd heard someone crying out.

"Hello?" Sue had called out into the darkness. "Is someone there? *Heeeeello?*"

After some time, she realized that one of the noisy machines was producing a vibration that sounded like *heeeeeelp meeeeee.*

Sue was beginning to crack. She'd been in the cell alone for several weeks, and her mind was weakening. They fed her just once a day, usually around dinnertime or a little later. From what she saw on her tray, it seemed they were serving her left-over slops from upstairs. Sometimes she'd find a slice of pizza that had already been bitten into; the milk or whatever beverage they brought was always open. She looked down and stared at the sac—the pus balloon—protruding from her gut. For the first time since arriving at Palisades, Susan Colt thought she might die there. Panic swirled inside her, the tension building in her nerves like a mounting cyclone. No one interacted with her anymore. It was as if they had forgotten her, allowing her to slowly decay until she was eventually taken by infection or star-vation. Her mind raced through the terrible ways she could die, and the panic grew exponentially. She held up her arms, then studied her legs. She'd definitely lost weight. It was hard to say without a mirror, but she guessed she was down fifteen, twenty pounds. She nestled back on the cot. God, it would be another sleepless night, she ruminated. The pain was unbearable.

A few minutes passed before the lights flooded the cell. Sue heard the clicking of heels and groaned as the bright fluo-rescents assaulted her eyes. Just as she was beginning to get some shut-eye—having finally ignored the pain enough for her mind to drift toward a dream—she was awakened. *Now what?*

"Hi, there, dear."

It was Silvaine Davies. What the fuck did the bitch want at this hour? Sue was irritable, the pain in her midsection felt like razor blades slicing at her stomach tissue. She remained in a left lateral recumbent position and did not turn, continuing to stare at the cracks in the wall.

"That's not how you should greet your queen."

"You're no queen," Sue spat. "You're a scum-sucking whore."

"Is that so? Look at me before I punish you."

Sue rotated and looked at her. The smirk Davies gave her made her skin crawl. It was the sort of smile a psychopath might wear, and it did a poor job of hiding her depraved nature.

"We'll see who's the whore." Davies slid a long, black object through the bars. It flopped to the floor, landing near the center of the cell.

Sue stared at it. "What's that?"

"You have eyes, don't you? Take a look at it. Pick it up."

Sue crawled off the cot and nudged it with her toe. "Is that a sex toy?

"Ding, ding, ding! So you're not as stupid as you look."

Sue backed away from it, returning to her cot. "I want to be left alone. Please. I'm in a lot of pain. I just want to rest." The exertion and movement were making the pain worse.

"Let's make a deal. You do something for me, and I'll give you these." Davies held up her open palm, revealing several white pills. "They'll take the pain away immediately. I promise you. Take these, and you won't feel a thing for the rest of the night."

Sue locked in on the pills. She wanted them—needed them. "What do you want me to do?"

Take that dildo and start using it.

"Fuck you."

"If that's how you want to play it, then so be it. You can

suffer silently. And frankly, I don't care if you die." Davies turned to go.

"Wait…"

The older woman stopped and turned slowly. "Are you going to do what I ask? You want the pain to end, don't you?"

Sue hesitated. The pain was extreme to the point where she thought she might vomit. "How long?" Sue asked.

"How long what?"

"How long do you want me to use the dildo for?"

"Oh, just a few minutes. I've got things to do, Susan. I'm quite busy and I don't have all night." Davies's eyes seemed to light up. "Are you going to play with it?"

"Yes," Sue said, feeling defeated. She had no other option. She needed those painkillers like a heroin addict needs her H. She staggered toward the dildo and picked it up. It felt awkward and heavy in her hand.

"Go to the cot. I want you to spread your legs and I want to see you insert it in your vagina."

"It's really big." Sue's voice trembled. "What if it doesn't fit?"

"Use this." Davies tossed a small bottle into her cell. When Sue got a good look at it, she realized what it was. Lubricant. *Fuck.* She returned to the cot and sat down. *Maybe it would be better if I just died,* she thought suddenly. *This is hell. If there is a hell, it's the Palisades Academy in the sublevel basement, and Silvaine Davies is Lucifer.* She opened her legs and splashed some of the lube onto herself. Closing her eyes, she began to rub the oversized dildo against her body. She could barely get the tip in. Several sobs harrowed her; she had no idea how she was going to fit that damned thing inside. She'd watched a video clip once with Pat and Doug of a man and a woman doing the deed. They'd glimpsed it for twenty seconds, then giggled and clicked out of it. She knew where to place it. The problem was it was just too big—impossibly big for her.

"Come on, you can do it. It'll enter. Just keep getting wet."

Davies's voice sounded sultry. Watching Sue play with herself was obviously turning her on. "That's it. You're a doll. You're so sexy, Susan."

Davies's voice made her nervous, and she tightened up. She tried to tune it out. She needed those pills, and if this was what it took to get them, then so be it. She squeezed more lube onto herself and kept rubbing the huge phallus against her vaginal opening.

"That's it, baby. Oh, you're *so* sexy."

Sue glanced up and it looked like the older woman had dropped her pants and slipped her fingers beneath her panties to play with herself. Davies moaned, savoring the erotic and perverse tableau.

The dildo finally slipped in.

"Ow, damn!" Sue shrieked. She slowly pumped the object in and out, in and out. Closing her eyes, she moaned and shrieked with every insertion. The pain was real. "Oh, my God."

"Does that feel good, baby? Oh, I bet it feels good, doesn't it?" Davies's eyes were rolled toward the back of her head. She jammed her fingers into herself, her hand clapping against her skin with relentless intensity making a clapping sound.

She let the dildo drop to the floor, crying now.

"You're a fucking evil cunt, you know that?" she wailed.

Davies pulled her pants up and clipped her belt. "And you're a sexy little whore. There'll be another time to play. Oh, I can't wait to play with you," Davies said excitedly. "Your vagina gets so wet. I can't wait to taste it." She dropped the pills on the ground on Sue's side of the bars.

Sue wrapped herself in the shabby blanket and turned away from Davies, letting out painful, pitiful sobs. Her body shuddered. "Go away. Leave me alone!"

"Just one more thing before I leave you, Susan. We'll have some visitors tomorrow. I'm going to bring you upstairs.

You'll be heavily medicated and no one will speak to you, but you may see some of your old friends. Make sure to ignore them." Davies sighed. "I really wish I could just leave you down here. It would really make things a lot easier. But you're still technically enrolled here as a patient, and if you're not present during the visit and they ask about you—" she took a deep breath "—well, that wouldn't be good, now, would it?"

Susan whispered, "I'm going to kill you." She said it low and was far enough away from Davies that she hadn't heard her.

"Practice with the dildo. You've got the lube there, and after a few more attempts, it should start to feel pleasurable rather than painful." Davies turned and her heels clicked down the dim corridor. "I left your pills on the floor." Her voice trailed away. "Make sure to take them before the rats chew them up."

Sue threw herself off the cot and scrambled to find the pills on the floor. She grabbed them just as she heard the door shut behind Davies; a moment later, the lights went out. She swallowed the pills. Her throat was dry, and now, aside from the intense pain in her gut, she felt a burning heat in her vagina.

Within ten minutes, the pills began to dull the agony, and it wasn't long before she drifted into a dreamless sleep.

Bex had just come in from the yard the following afternoon when she spotted Sue in the TV room. Two guards flanked her, and a counselor pushed her in a wheelchair.

"Holy shit," Bex said, staring in a daze of incredulity.

Christine hurried over. They were in the lounge, and a pair of glass-paned doors separated them from the TV room. "I can't believe it. Is that..." Christine said.

"It's fucking Sue. I knew she was still here."

"Me, too," Christine replied. "Why is she dressed like that?"

"Something's so, *so* wrong," Bex said, shaking her head. "Look at her. What have they done to her?"

It was difficult to get a good look at her, but Bex could see Sue had lost weight. She looked frail even with the heavy coat they'd put on her. They'd dressed her in a winter coat, wrapped a scarf around her, and put a beanie on her head. She wore a pair of hideous sunglasses—the kind Bex had seen her grandmother wear during the summer. Cataract glasses. What the hell was going on? Sue looked like Bernie in *Weekend at Bernie's*. A lifeless prop that mimicked her once vibrant, effervescent self.

"I have to talk to her," Bex said, making her way toward the television room. Christine attempted to grab her arm, but she shook her off.

"There's security in there," Christine warned.

When she was near the doors, the guards had turned and met her gaze, blocking her entry.

"You can't come in here," one of the guards yelled through the doors.

"What? Why not?"

"She just had an operation and can't be near anyone," the counselor cut in. "Her immune system is in a vulnerable state."

"But I want to talk to her."

"Sorry, it's not happening."

Bex stood staring at her old friend through the window panes. Sue's head was tilted down. She looked like she may have been asleep. *What'd they do to her?* She returned to the common area, her face flushed, looking like a scarlet ghost.

"What'd they say?" Christine asked.

"They won't let me go near her."

"Why in the hell not?"

"Apparently she just had an operation, and it has something to do with her immune system."

"That's absolute bullshit."

"I know." Bex stared at the stone-faced guards, who stood garrisoned around Sue, preventing the other patients from coming near her. "They did something to her. They're keeping her somewhere… She's still here in the facility, somewhere."

Christine frowned at her. "This place might be more fucked than we initially thought."

With anger rising inside of her, Bex turned and saw a horde of superiors enter the common room. Silvaine Davies led them in, appearing to give a personal tour of Palisades. These must be the officials from the state. Today, the old woman was all smiles, looking elegant in her two thousand dollar suit. Bex could tell the tribunal members inspecting the facility on this momentous day were beguiled by Davies. She was a con woman, and they were eating up her story. From the look on their faces, they seemed pleased by what they saw. Everyone had fallen for the act—the parents, the guardians, the public—and now the state seemed persuaded by her masquerade. Bex had to do something. But what? At least Christine finally saw the truth of what she'd suspected for some time. The two of them could figure out, somehow, how to reach Sue and help her.

Susan Colt stirred in the wheel chair. A deep drowse and grogginess made her head feel heavy like it was filled with lead. Someone was pushing her through a corridor. They'd placed dark sunglasses over her eyes, but she could tell the lighting was different. She realized she was upstairs. *I'm upstairs with the others! They could help me!*

"Help!" she croaked.

"She's awake," someone said from behind her.

"Help me!"

"Shit…"

Someone wrapped a piece of foul-smelling cloth around her mouth and gagged her. She started to regain feeling in her limbs and writhed in the chair. Sue shuddered and panted. They'd strapped her to the chair, and her terror mounted when she realized she couldn't get free.

"Stop it!" someone barked, then she was struck hard in the back of her head.

Sue let out a painful cry. Someone had punched her.

"We need to get her into health services now," the counselor ordered. "She's waking up."

"Let's go," someone else blurted.

They wheeled her rapidly out of the common area. The bottom of the wheelchair and her feet crashed through a door and she was driven into the medical room. There was a doctor waiting, wearing a mask. He stood stolidly—a functionary merely following orders—brandishing a syringe tipped with a three-inch needle.

Oh, God. No!

They hoisted her off the chair and laid her down in the supine position atop the examination table. Her shirt was raised. The doctor peered over her and she felt the needle pierce through her stomach, directly in the area where her pustule was. The golf ball sac filled with fluid burst, and the needle was driven into the deep tissue.

Sue screamed in agony.

A guard grabbed her under her back and tossed her back onto the wheelchair. They placed the cataract glasses over her eyes and she was rushed out of medical. A long trip through a corridor brought her to the elevator and it descended quickly to the sublevel. Though it was difficult to see through the dark tint of the sunglasses, Sue tried to observe her surroundings, making mental notes of the facility as she passed through it. She was wading through sectors of Palisades she'd never seen before.

When the elevator opened, the corridor seemed to stretch into darkness. A light panel would come on every ten feet or so, triggered by motion, as they moved along. The underground area was much larger than she'd imagined. Sue's heart jackhammered in her chest as she was pushed down the long passageway. She glimpsed cells, much like her own, on the left side. Toward the middle of the corridor, Sue saw a girl locked inside one of the cells. Her face looked haggard—a skinny little thing, half-naked. She looked up from her cot and met Sue's gaze just as Sue wheeled past her. She shuddered at her grim site: a depleted sack of flesh and bones.

"Hey…" Sue muttered. Whatever they'd injected her with had begun to dull her mind and movements.

"Help me." The girl's voice was a wisp—a faint wind rattling the leaves on a dying branch—as Sue was carted onward.

Sue was unconscious by the time they returned her to her cell.

CHAPTER
EIGHT

LATER AT DINNER, Bex and Christine had wrangled a few of the girls and explained to the ones who had never met Sue, having arrived after she went missing, who she was. Julie, Christine's roommate, listened intently, along with Sarah, Bex's roommate, and a few others. Bex had their attention when she began telling them about the Safe Room. Some of the girls had just arrived that week and had not yet been subjected to the tortures of the Safe Room. Their eyes opened wide and their attention was tuned in on Bex's accounts of what went on within the walls of Palisades.

"So, that girl with the thick grandma glasses in the TV room," Mia began, "You thought she'd been discharged?"

"Yeah, that's what they told us," Bex replied. "We haven't seen her in almost two months. Not since July."

"Seriously? That's fucking insane," Mia said.

"This place isn't what you think it is. Believe nothing you hear, ladies," Bex cautioned.

The girls stared at her, soaking in her intensity. Judging by their reactions, Bex gathered they were convinced and frightened by the stories they were told.

"They claim that what they do here is for our betterment,"

Christine added. "All they do is torture us—mentally and physically." She sighed.

"She didn't look too good," Mia commented. "That giant coat did a poor job trying to hide it, but she looked pretty gaunt."

"We need to rescue her," Bex said with conviction. "We need to find out where they're hiding her and get the fuck out of here."

"I'm in," Mia said.

"Me too," a lanky girl blurted.

"I wanna help, too," Julie, Christine's roommate, chimed.

The gang was assembling. Bex looked at the girls closely, assessing their potential. Some of them looked tough. A few of them might get the shit kicked out of them. The lanky girl didn't have a shot. But maybe she had something crazy inside of her she could channel, and it could be useful when the time came. Their rage had been building for a while now, even before they got to the Palisades Academy. Bex could see the girls' fire blazing in their eyes. The type of fire that could spark dynamite and blow through a mountain. There was something there, Bex had realized. All their lives, these girls were told they were fuck-ups: trash, scum, degenerates. Many of them had been exposed to drugs and alcohol at a young age. They'd grown up in abusive households with insane parents. Raised by single parents, foster parents, parents who weren't present. Parents who were present but checked out. Some were sexually abused at a young age. Fucked and sodomized by relatives, babysitters, older kids in the neighborhood. Bex stared at the girls. These were *her* girls—her comrades. They were finally going to fight back. Fight the establishment—the motherfuckers—who've been putting them down their entire lives. Bex clenched her fists. She was breathing hard.

"I have an idea—" Bex began.

"Let's all get tatted, bitches!" Andrea interrupted.

"Yes!" Mia said, excitedly.

Bex frowned. "People, we have to stay focused on the task at hand—"

"Oh, my god. I've been wanting a tattoo since forever," Christine said in a high voice. "You draw real good, right?"

"Real well," Bex corrected. "It's real well, not real good." But nobody seemed to hear her. The new girl, Andrea, had already enthralled the group with her good looks and smooth-talking demeanor. To make matters worse, it appeared Christine was fawning all over her. *Pretty-faced bitch.* They were laughing at her quips and had taken a liking to her. Bex hated her already and was likely fixing her with a mean scowl, but she tried to relax her face. Now was not the time to make enemies, she reminded herself. She had to avoid conflict and rally the troops if they were going to save Sue. There was strength in numbers; if Bex created a rift amongst the girls, finding and saving Sue would grind to a halt. So, she shut her mouth and went along with the inanities that the others were engaging in. At least for the time being.

Silvaine sat at her desk. The two officials from the state sat down opposite her. She was used to working in high-pressure environments and felt confident things had gone as smoothly as possible during the visit, but a nagging feeling left her wondering—what if they'd seen something? Paranoia began to swirl inside her gut. Sweat tricked down the back of her neck. *Had they noticed something odd about Sue?*

"Mrs. Davies—" the chubby, balding bureaucrat began. He glanced down at his notes. He, along with the jowly woman who had a face that reminded Davies of cottage cheese, held clipboards, glancing down at them on occasion. They focused on their notes and exchanged reticent glances, making Silvaine nervous. "We all agree—" he began, but then stopped with another awkward pause.

What the fuck is up with these people? Davies thought bitterly. She expected them to have long sticks up their asses, but she'd also gathered they were gauche cretins on top of it. Completely unaware of any social cues.

"—that the Palisades Academy for Young Women and Teens—"

"Is a markedly exceptional institution," cheese face cut in. "We can tell you are doing great things here, Mrs. Davies. Magnificent things!" The old crag was ecstatic.

Davies's face lit up. She then became elated herself. *Phew. Guess it had gone well after all.*

"Yes, yes," the bald man said. "Quite magnificent, if I must say. These young women are in great hands. They couldn't be at a better place."

"Hell, I'd stay here if—"

"Harv, that's enough," the old woman barked.

He dropped his head in shame.

"There is one thing I'm wondering about," she continued.

"Yes?"

"The young girl who had eye surgery."

Uh-oh.

"She doesn't look too good. Is she eating?"

"Oh, that poor thing," Davies replied. "She was suffering from strabismus. One eye was pointing this way, the other that-a-way." She pointed in opposite directions and crossed her eyes. "The extraocular muscle surgery took a toll on her. But she *is* getting better." Silvaine could feel her heart thumping in her chest. She hoped they'd move past the subject and continue to extol the Academy for her wonderful work and leadership.

The bald man's head was glistening with sweat. It was clear he hardly walked or exerted himself much physically, and they'd been touring the grounds for over two hours. He and the crone beside him nodded their heads slowly, as if ruminating deeply about their analysis of either Susan Colt, or the Academy as a whole.

"Is there anything else you have questions about?" Davies asked. "Would you like to see any medical records?"

"No, that isn't necessary, Mrs. Davies," the crone answered. "I believe we've seen everything we intended to." She shot the heavyset man a look of approval and sat up. "I must say, Mrs. Davies, we are blown away by your system and we'd like to commend you with all that you're doing for these young girls." Her mouth curved into a semblance of a small smile for the first time during their visit. "It's clear you and your team are going above and beyond to help these children. Because that's what they still are. They're children and they need all the help they can get. Clearly you are delivering that, and we congratulate you on all your hard work." The old crone stuck out her hand and shook with Davies. "It clearly shows," she added.

It was a struggle for Silvaine Davies not to break out in laughter. "We take great pride in what we do at Palisades— our caring staff is carefully appointed. This all wouldn't be possible if it weren't for our amazing staff, and our board who supports our efforts without reservation." She signaled to the CEO, Albert Weer, and William Dunkle, the Academy's CFO. They'd remained quiet during the visit, William only speaking about some of the numbers and costs for the therapies when asked. He made sure not to divulge more information than was necessary, and only proffered what was requested. "It was our pleasure having you visit."

The crone and bald man said their goodbyes and left the office. Davies could relax now and looked at her right hand, which was shaking unsteadily, as the door closed behind the state bureaucrats. Weer, who was standing next to her, seemed to notice and gave her a curious look.

~

Susan Colt awoke into a world of crippling nausea.

"Fuck..." she said, rolling to her right side. "*Ah...Damn*," she gasped.

She needed to use the bucket, but it was so far away. Oh, Christ, it was on another planet. She'd used it already several times and it hadn't been cleaned. She wondered if they'd forgotten about her. She'd perish in her own rot and stink, down in the bowels of the Palisades Academy for Young Women and Teens. The place her godawful parents had sent her to. They'd sent her to die! *Rehabilitation my ass!* With every passing second, she became more resentful toward her mom and dad. Maybe they wanted her to die. What if they had gotten to the point where they figured there was no chance anyone could fix her? Or, they simply grew tired of caring for her, and this was the easiest alternative? Just send your kids to death camp.

She shifted in her cot and shuddered. The pain was concentrated in her midsection where the needle had been lodged. Her mind flashed grisly images of the doctor and his syringe. Doctor death.

She touched the area lightly and the pain shot immediately through her midsection, shocking her nerves. Remaining recumbent, she kept still or else the pain would jolt her. Tears began to cloud her vision.

"Fucking, dammit," she muttered to the void.

Desperation began to wrap its ugly tendrils around her spirit and strangle her usually buoyant perspective. It wasn't only the shooting pain that had knocked the girl's spirits down into the doldrums. It was the sight of the pus sac that had been popped and shriveled into a nauseating flap of skin, now hanging loose, that sucked all optimism from her. Perhaps this was the end of things, and she would die after all, at the sadistic hands of Silvaine Davies.

She stared at the metal bars that enclosed her. There was no getting out through the heavy-duty bolted door. Not even a gorilla could bust through the bars. Someone would have to let her out. Or, she'd have to attempt to escape when someone, namely Davies, entered her cage.

Sue tried to stifle the hammering pain. In the cold darkness, and through the din of the HVAC system and clanging pipes, she heard a wispy voice cry out, "Please, help me." It took her a moment to remember who it was. That poor girl, she thought. Who knew how long she'd been detained down in the Palisades dungeon. Hysteria began to overwhelm her psyche as the realization that, she too, may end up like the emaciated girl.

Andrea stabbed the needle into Christine's thigh.

Bex was watching through a gap in the shower curtain. Frowning.

"Ahh," Christine yelped.

"Shhhhhhh," Andrea said. "We can't make any noise."

"I'll try not to. It hurts, though."

Andrea had rigged an electric toothbrush and had jimmied a sharp needle to the end, creating a jailhouse tattoo gun.

They were crammed in a shower stall in the girl's bathroom. Andrea drilled the needle in, applying ink. Her brow scrunched in a V-shape of intense concentration toward the task at hand. After an hour and fifteen minutes of labor, she'd already drawn a tribal-style owl.

"Fuuuuuck," Christine gasped.

"Shut the hell up, Christine," Andrea ordered. "We get caught in here doing this, we're fucked."

"Okay, okay."

Bex hated that the design was coming out splendid. The

girl was a tremendous artist, and the fact was undeniable. She couldn't believe how with only a primitive, makeshift tool, Andrea was able to design such a masterful tattoo.

"I might have to stop soon after I finish the outline…"

"Okay…"

"Let's go, c'mon," Bex hurried them on. "Dinner's in fifteen. We should get going."

"Chill, I just gotta finish this little…" Andrea bit her lip, focusing hard, "this little line… here."

"We're gonna get caught," Bex grumbled.

Andrea stopped the makeshift tattoo gun and turned to her. "Bitch, you can go if you want. You don't have to babysit us."

Bex, who was a pacifist and normally didn't have an ounce of aggression in her, suddenly felt the urge to strangle Andrea.

The two girls locked eyes. Bex's face flushed red as the anger inside her rose. She stopped herself from acting and potentially making a grave mistake.

"You're nothing but a cheap slut," Bex spat, then stormed out of the bathroom.

Back in her room, Bex plopped herself on her bed, face first and screamed into her pillow. "*Ahhhhhhhhh!*" The sound was muffled but had rattled Sarah.

"Are you all right, Rebecca?"

Why can't she call me Bex? Goddamnit! Bex hated when people called her Rebecca. She had such a cool nickname, and it was spoiled when some bloke decided to call her by her birth name. She'd decided when she turned eighteen, she was going to legally change her name to Bex.

"Rebecca…"

Bex turned around and laid on her back, removing the pillow from her face. "Can you please call me Bex. We've been through this a million times. I hate the name Rebecca. Is it so difficult to do that?

"I just don't understand how Bex is short for Rebecca. I don't get it."

"Ughhhh… you don't have to get it. But that's what I prefer. Can you just be a sport and go with the flow?"

"Fine…"

Bex shot up out of bed and paced around the room. Now was not the time to get all depressed and down in the dumps. She thought of Sue and how she was in some very serious peril. Screw Christine, she thought. If she wanted to get with the new girl, then so be it. There were more important matters at hand. Bex glanced over at Sarah who was staring back at her curiously.

"Wanna try my vape?" Sarah asked.

Bex wasn't sure if she heard her right. There was no way Sarah had a vape. She was a goody two-shoes—a rule follower—who wouldn't dare break any code.

"Huh?" was all Bex could think to respond. "You have a vape?"

"Yup."

"No fucking way."

"Yes way, dolly. So, you wanta hit it?" Sarah smirked at her. "Or, you gonna just stand around like a square?"

"In our room? Shouldn't we go somewhere?"

"No one's coming. They checked the room already. We're clear 'till morning."

"Yeah?"

Sarah nodded. She slipped the little vape into Bex's hand. "Pace yourself. It's really good stuff. Strong. And if I'm not mistaken, you haven't done it in a while."

Bex took the vape and turned away from the door. She crouched near the corner of the room and took a few tokes. Small puffs of smoke billowed, filling Bex's lungs, making her cough.

Sarah laughed from her bed. "You've turned into a light-weight again, huh?"

Bex made her way back to Sarah and furtively passed her the vape. "Shit, yeah. I guess it's been a while since mine died." She coughed again. "Going on two months now. Maybe a little longer." Then, suddenly, a random thought popped into her head. "Where'd you get it from?"

"You know that creep, Jack?"

"The counselor?" Bex's eyes were glassy and wide.

"Yeah. He gave it to me."

"What? You're kidding!"

"I swear on my mother's grave." She then burst out laughing.

"What's so goddamn funny?"

"Sorry… My mom's already dead. I have to swear on… something else."

"Quit it, Sarah. Where'd you get the vape from?"

"From Jack. He gave it to me."

Bex studied her, unsure if she was toying with her.

"All I had to do was give him a BJ."

Her eyes opened wide and her jaw dropped. "You what?"

"You know, a blow job."

"Damnit, Sarah, I know what a fucking blow job is! I'm not a square." Bex cringed, thinking to herself that she had spent too much time with Christine's roommate, Julie, and had picked up her ridiculous vernacular. "What I'd like to know is *why* you gave him a BJ?"

"So that I could get the pot. I wanted the vape."

"Oh, my god…" Bex paced around the room, clutching ropes of her hair. She was beyond frustrated and would have to drop the subject or else she'd lose it. "Are you always this dense?"

"There's something else I need to tell you…"

Bex glanced up at her. They stared at each other for a long moment, until Bex finally said, "Well? What do you need to tell me?"

"Jack told me where they're keeping her."

"Keeping who?" Bex blurted. "What the hell are you talking about?"

"Where they're keeping Sue."

Bex could feel her heart racing in her chest. She seemed to have forgotten to breathe because after a few seconds, she was panting for air. Her mind was moving a million miles per hour. "Sarah, what the fuck are you talking about?"

"So, me and Jack, well… we talk." She sighed. "This isn't the first time I've done something for him." She took a puff from her vape then hid it underneath her pillow. "We've gotten kinda… close."

"Holy shit, Sarah. Can you let me know what's going on? Where are they keeping her?" Bex was at her wits' end. She thought in another moment she'd charge her roommate and begin shaking her, forcing the information out of her. "C'mon. Out with it! You need to tell me what you know."

"Okay…" Sarah leaned forward and lowered her voice. Bex moved closer to listen to what she was about to say. "There's secret places here. Hidden places only a few people know about. Some of the staff apparently don't even know about it." She cleared her throat. "There's like a secret dungeon underneath the building. And there's all sorts of weird, evil shit that goes on there."

Bex said nothing.

"Crazy stuff, huh?"

Bex stared at her roommate, thinking how her suspicions were confirmed by what she was told—that Palisades is an evil place, and if they don't do something, Sue might not make it out alive.

Down in the Palisades dungeon, Davies entered Susan Colt's cell. There were a few others with the director today, and that surprised Sue. She didn't think many others besides Davies and Jack, and maybe another counselor or nurse, knew about her and The Ghost Girl. Sue referred to the other girl as The Ghost Girl because she never saw her (besides that one fleeting time she skirted past in the wheelchair), but she'd hear her calling for help every now and then in her wispy, haunting voice. But at the end of the day, it didn't surprise Sue so many of them—so many of the screws—were evil freaks, and possible devil-worshippers. On this day, Davies was accompanied by Jack, Carmen, the female nurse, the doctor (Doctor Death), and a nerdy-looking man in a Brooks Brothers button down shirt and nice slacks who looked like a big shot.

Beads of sweat dribbled down Sue's face, her hair soggy clumps of rope. She'd developed a high fever and felt extremely sick the past few days. She guessed they were all there due to her looking rather ill.

"Susan," Davies began. "The doctor is here to examine you."

Sue could see the crone's evil, beady eyes through the cold beams of light that shot into her cell. They were black eyes that belonged to a witch, she thought.

"Please," she continued. "Don't give him any trouble. He's here to help you. We want to help you get better."

Sue didn't respond. She felt so sick and was zapped of all her energy. Her burn wound had definitely gotten infected, and that was most likely their primary concern and reason for being there. The skin flap had turned into necrotic tissue, and beneath it her open wound looked like spoiled, rotted flesh.

She groaned in pain. Something had to be done sooner rather than later, she knew—or she'd die from infection. It was a no-brainer.

The doctor, an impersonal, draconian-type, unveiled a syringe and stepped toward her. "This may hurt a tad. But it's for your own benefit, to stop the infection from spreading."

"Please…" Sue muttered, groggily.

The doctor plunged the needle into her wound and she yelped.

"We had to do something, Susan," Davies said from the doorway. "We couldn't just allow you to suffer like that. Hopefully the medicine works quickly. I want to see you healthy and spry again." She smiled at Sue, who lay hunched over clutching her stomach, grimacing and panting.

The doctor moved her arm and shot her with another syringe.

"*Ahhhhh… oooo… ahhhh!*"

"This one is for the pain," the doctor said. "There, there," he consoled her, and patted her on her damp forehead. He held out his hand, and in his right palm there were two white pills. "Take these."

It took all the energy inside her, but Sue opened her mouth and swallowed them.

He shoved a water bottle in her mouth and she took a large gulp. "Antibiotics to combat the infection," he added, then withdrew, appearing shaken from the sight of her. Perhaps he thought she might drop dead in his presence.

Sue looked up at them, and through cloudy tears, she saw the stone-faced bastards. They were staring at her as if she were some freakish attraction in a zoo or a carnival. *Ladies and gentlemen, step right up for your chance to see Torture Girl, where you can poke, prod, fuck, humiliate, and do whatever you want to her. Come one, come all! Mature audiences only…children under the age of sixteen should proceed with caution, and be accompanied by an adult.*

"I'll be back soon to check up on you," Davies said.

Click-click-click-click

The clatter of Davies's heels echoed down the huge passageway, as Sue lay clutching her stomach protectively, hoping she could ride out the infection and the pain. In the midst of her agony, she had enough awareness and fortitude to promise to herself she would not allow herself to die in the hands of Davies and her goons.

CHAPTER
NINE

CHRISTINE SAW NOTHING BUT BLACK. They'd tied a blindfold around her head. She took in a labored breath and exhaled. The sessions had gotten stranger and more twisted since she'd begun Phase 2 of her "recovery". The last thing on earth she was doing, she reflected, was recovering. She was waiting eagerly for the session to reach the climax, where she'd be shamed and flogged. At least after that, she knew she'd basically be done for the evening.

"Tell the group your sins, Chrissy." It was Jillian, the counselor who impelled her to disclose her innermost secrets. She was effective at it, too. Jill had become a master inquisitor, able to make even the most stubborn souls squirm under her scrutiny.

"WELL?" Jill shouted. The little lady could really make her voice boom! "Out with it already. We know you've sinned. God knows you've sinned."

Shit. Have to think of something. There was that new girl, Mia, who thought she was tough and told Jill she hadn't sinned, and had remained firm in her assertion, not budging in the least. Jill flogged the living crap out of her. Christine and the others who witnessed it were left speechless, shaking with gut-twisting fear.

Christine could still hear the rods smacking violently against the girl's buttocks. The sound was imprinted in her mind.

CRAAAACK. CRAACK. CRACK.

Mia, poor girl, who's five foot nothing, and ninety-something pounds, couldn't sit down for a week. The rods had drawn blood, and the girls present, including Christine, Andrea, and Julie, were cautioned not to speak of what they witnessed. If they did, they were told… Well, they were told the punishment for talking about any of the disciplining was worse than what they'd witnessed according to Jillian.

"Christine!" Jill's shrieking voice snapped her back to the present. "Tell the group how you've sinned. NOW!"

"I had lustful thoughts," she blurted. *Can't think of anything else, dammit. Have to say something. Gotta think quick now.*

"About whom?"

"Jack…"

"Our Jack?" Her question was drawn out, her tone dripping with a flabbergasted incredulity.

She hesitated for a moment, then replied: "Yes." She wasn't sure if she'd just made a huge mistake.

"Interesting," Jillian said, with obvious sarcasm. "That's very interesting, Christine."

Christine heard the faint sounds of shuffling in the room and whispering.

"No one said you can talk!" Jill yelled, scolding the other girls. "So, Christine. As penance for your sins—namely lust—you have two options. The first is you can elect flogging. Ten strikes by yours truly. The second option—you can taste Jack."

The room fell silent. Someone gasped.

"I'm sorry. Taste Jack?" Christine asked. She was confused.

"I'll allow you to kiss him. If that's what you really want. Yes, yes—" she was speaking fast now, "—I'll allow you to act on your desires. It'll be between you and God. I've got no part in the matter. *Why* end at lust, whore, when you can go all the way?"

"I..."

"Shut up! Take off your clothes."

Christine remained frozen, blindfolded and dazed. None of this seemed real. She figured she'd dozed off and was moored in a very lucid nightmare.

"NOW!" Jillian yelled.

She removed her top and her bottoms. Left with only her panties and the blindfold, a chill spread through her body. She hugged her breasts attempting to warm herself. Fear gripped her like a convict's climb to the gallows. She wished she could crawl into a hole in the wall and hide.

"Take a look girls. A real Jezebel," Jillian scoffed.

Christine was smacked on her shoulder with a rod. She screamed.

"Kneel!"

Christine dropped to her knees, the blindfold still wrapped on her face, but she was crying now.

"Jack," Jillian ordered, "give her a taste. And the rest of you will watch."

There was more whispering and a sinister electricity seemed to enfold the small room.

Christine's head was lifted, and Jack said, "Open your mouth." The eagerness in his voice made her cringe.

Through tears and whimpers, she opened her mouth and felt hard flesh slip inside. He'd thrusted his penis in her mouth. It was large and solid. He pushed it deeper and deeper and she gagged.

"Suck it..."

She complied.

"That's it…" he moaned.

"You have to watch!" Jillian bellowed. She was addressing the other girls, forcing them to watch.

Underneath her blindfold, Christine performed oral sex on Jack. Her actions were automatic. As she pleasured him, she stifled her emotions, removing herself from the act entirely. She separated herself psychologically from the situation, tricking her mind and imagining she was somewhere else.

The next morning, Bex caught up to Christine on the breakfast line in the cafeteria.

"Hey, how've you been?" Bex asked. "I haven't seen you in a few days." During Phase 2 of recovery, the girls were separated for longer periods of time. The "meditation" sessions were more drawn out and more intense, and the counselors argued that such psychic realignment was required for their recovery—for their benefit. Since Bex and Christine had been separated into different groups, Bex didn't see her friend as often and she missed her soft smile.

Christine's head was tilted down as she moved along on the breakfast line, sliding her tray. Her eyes looked sad and she ambled along listlessly, barely noticing Bex's presence. Something's wrong, Bex thought.

"Chrissy, you all right?" she asked. "What's the matter?"

Christine tilted her head up and just shook her head, offering no response.

They'd arrived in front of the cafeteria attendant, who served Christine and then Bex a ladleful of curdled powdered eggs. Bex's stomach churned at the sight of them.

"Gross," she muttered. "Why are you ignoring me? Can you tell me what's going on?"

Suddenly, Andrea appeared out of nowhere and stepped

in between them. She got right in Bex's face. *"Don't* talk to her, Rebecca!" Andrea snapped.

"What the hell?"

"She's going through a lot right now, and you don't need to make it worse for her."

"How am I—"

"Just stay the hell away from her. Okay?" Andrea stared down into Bex's eyes. They looked mean and crazy, and Bex didn't want to push her. She got the hint.

"Fine… I just wanted to see if she was okay," Bex said, her voice trembling. *God, why am I so intimidated by this nutjob.* She thinks she's so goddamn high and mighty. Embarrassed by the interaction, Bex took her tray, grabbed a bottle of orange juice, and retreated into the cafeteria. She was crushed that Christine didn't defend her and had barely even glanced at her. *Some friend,* she thought, as she searched the caf for familiar faces.

She spotted Sarah and Chatterbox already seated at a table, accompanied by a few other girls, and made her way over.

"Hiya, Bex," Sarah greeted her.

Bex tried to shrug off her frustrated feelings with Christine, but it was hard to get her mind off of her. She kept glancing over at Chrissy and Andrea. They were sharing a bottle of orange juice with two straws, and Chrissy was laughing at something Andrea had said to her. Jealousy was consuming Bex like a gray cloud in an impending storm.

"Shit… really sorry she took your girl," Chatterbox murmured.

Bex wanted to respond that Andrea was a fake friend, and Christine would realize it soon enough, but she didn't have it in her. She simply kept quiet and stared listlessly at her ex-lover.

"She'll come back around," Sarah said. "You're way cooler than her. I can't believe she fell for that fucking cunt."

Abby muttered something but no one seemed to hear her. She spoke too softly and instead of asking her what she had said, the girls just carried on.

Sarah shot Bex a grave look. "I have some intel for you," she said. "You might not like it, though."

She'd had her full attention. "What is it?"

"Apparently Sue is really sick. The doctor's been treating her. She might have an infection or something like that."

"Oh, my god. What the hell are those bastards doing to her?"

"Jack told me Davies has made her…" Sarah stalled.

"Made her what?" Bex demanded. "What did that fucker say?"

Sarah turned her eyes away, too embarrassed to repeat what he'd told her.

"Are you going to tell me what he said?" Bex asked.

Sarah shook her head. "It's so terrible. This place is worse than what any of us could've imagined."

"We have to save her soon. Goddamnit!" Bex snapped.

"I might have a way we can get to her."

"Girls, this sounds very dangerous," Chatterbox cut in.

"No one asked your opinion, Chatterbox," Bex said. "And she was your roommate. How could you be so cold? You're okay knowing she's being held in some goddamn dungeon, and no one's doing a damn thing about it? Some loyalty you have."

"I want to save her as much as the rest of you, but what do you think will happen if any of us gets caught trying to look for her… in a restricted, off-limits part of the Academy. They are already crushing us, grinding us down slowly." Chatterbox looked down and her eyes turned sad. "Of course I want to help. I hope we can get her out of there. But do you think that's realistic?"

Bex realized maybe she was being too hard on the girl. They had all gone through so much torment at the hands of these awful people. Perhaps she had to adjust her approach, and that way, she could convince the girls they could be useful and serve a purpose; that there *was* hope, and they could help save Sue.

"Sarah, is there any way—any chance you could get a keycard? If we get our hands on that, we could have access to the elevators."

Sarah looked worried. "Mmmm. I don't know. That's risky." Her eyes panned across the caf and Bex followed her gaze. Jack was chatting with some new girls a few tables away. "I could try, but—"

"We need that keycard," Bex said. "Please…Can you work on it?"

~

"Hey, girlie… Hey…"

Sue turned on her cot. A flaring pain that was out of this world shot through her belly. She heard whispers again. Someone was calling out to her. Ghost Girl. But her voice sounded close, like she was just a few feet away. She must be dreaming, Sue figured, or just waking up from one.

"Hey, you awake?" the wispy voice asked. It was a little girl's voice. Only she sounded so close that it raised the hairs on the back of Sue's neck, and prompted her to sit up and check to see who was there.

"Hello?"

"It's me, your neighbor."

Sue shuddered as she took in the girl's grisly silhouette. Her ribs pressed against her and could be seen through the hollow cage of her chest. A bulb shining from far away made the grim spectacle even more unsettling. Her face was masked in shadows, and she could only see her discomforting outline.

The girl—if you could call her that—looked malnourished,

and the way she clung to the cell bars, as if she was a part of a carnival freak show, turned Sue's stomach into a knotted tangle. "What in the—" The girl's frightful outline scared her. If this was, in fact, Ghost Girl, how had she gotten *so* close to her? "Are you a ghost? This has to be a dream." Sue felt lightheaded.

"I'm not a ghost, silly. I'm real. As real as these steel bars." She rapped her knuckles on one of the metal bars. The sound of bone on steel echoing was all too real.

"I don't understand… How'd you get out of your cell?" Sue squinted and rubbed her eyes, making sure she wasn't looking at a mirage.

"I made a file with a spoon they gave me and I was able to bust out. It took a long time." She showed Sue the tool she'd contrived. It was long and pointy. The girl held it up and touched the sharp point to her finger. "Ah," she yelped. "Cut myself."

Sue stared, startled at the malformation standing before her, not understanding how a girl in such a state could act so *normal*.

Then she made a sucking *mmcht* sound with the side of her mouth, like she was sucking air and clicking the inside of her cheek. "But they don't know I can get out." The girl looked up and examined her surroundings. "At least I don't think they know. They probably would've done something about it by now if they did suspect something."

Sue wasn't sure what startled her more—the girl's lax demeanor, or her disfigured bone structure.

"Why haven't you escaped? Why are you still here?"

"I don't have a keycard… *yet*. You need a keycard to get back up. There's no way to get in the elevator, or use it without it."

"Davies," Sue muttered. "We need to come up with a plan."

A clattering noise made the girl's shoulders jump. Sue flinched at the sound. *Was it Davies coming down?*

The Ghost Girl let go of the bars and looked worried. "I'll be back soon, Susan," she whispered, then turned and scurried away.

"Wait!" Sue called after her. "You have to help me…" but the girl had already gone.

"I CAN'T TAKE it anymore! I can't take it!" Julie shouted.

"Julie! Please… you have to stop." Christine had been trying to calm her down for several minutes now, but she couldn't snap any reason into her. Any second now someone would appear and take her away—take her to the Safe Room. "You have to stop yelling."

Julie paced around the room. She clutched her hair and it made it messy. She'd torn at her clothes and she looked like a mental patient. "I'm going to kill myself, goddamnit! I'm going to end it once and for all. *AHHHHHHHHHHH!*"

"Julie! *Stop…* you're going to get in trouble." Christine was afraid she'd be implicated in the noise-making as well, but her pleas fell on deaf ears. She watched as her roommate reeled uncontrollably into a mania that she knew would be difficult, if not impossible, to come back from. "Knock it off, will you?" Then she heard banging on their door. Two security guards had appeared. It was only a matter of time before they heard the commotion. "Shit…"

They jostled into the room and the big one grabbed Julie by her wrists and forced her arms behind her back, then shoved her out of the room. The way they were handling her,

Christine wouldn't have been surprised if they dislocated her shoulder.

"You're in trouble now," the big one said.

She screamed like a wild animal on her way out.

"Shut up, will you?"

The other guard stared down Christine, making sure she didn't try anything. "Let me know if you need an extra hand."

"I got it handled," the big guard replied, as he manhandled her out of the room.

She writhed and flailed in his grasp, but he clamped down hard on her wrists. "Stop resisting," he ordered, then rammed his forearm into the back of her head.

She gasped, "Ah!" and staggered, almost tripping as she was steamrolled out of the room.

"Crap," Christine muttered to herself. She wanted to find Andrea and tell her what had happened but it was almost lights out. Not wanting to risk getting in trouble, she had no other choice but to wait until morning. Things were beginning to unfold rapidly. She closed her eyes and an unwelcome breath choked her, pressing into her fragile lungs like a heavy, invisible mass. A few quick flashes of sliced skin entered her mind. *God. Not now.* It was a portent—and a god-awful one at that. There was a shard of glass dripping with blood. The blood was fresh and she could see the sinews in the girl's wrists. "Stop," Christine said to herself. "Stop it!" She wanted to shut down the images that were assaulting her mind, but they kept coming—kept barraging her delicate mind like an endless rain in a deluge.

The next morning, after breakfast, Christine walked along the track. Though it was already fall, and the weather had gotten cooler, they still allowed the girls an hour of daily recreation if the weather permitted. One of her few solaces these days, Christine ruminated. The sun was strong and the heat was comforting as it warmed her face. The images of a girl bleeding from her wrists haunted her, even as she tried to brush off the macabre thoughts. Though she didn't want to acknowledge it, she knew damn well it was a portent.

"Hey, sexy," Andrea called out to her.

Christine stopped and turned, and waited for her friend to catch up to her. "Hey."

"Don't sound so thrilled." Andrea looked at her in a way that told Christine she knew something had happened. There was no hiding how dispirited she felt. She simply didn't want to discuss it. Not with Andrea or anyone else for that matter.

"Why the sad face?" Andrea asked, stretching out her fingers and stroking Christine's hand.

She breathed deeply, then replied, "They took Julie last night. She was manic. The poor girl…"

"Aw, dammit, Chrissy." She squeezed her hand. "I'm so sorry. What happened? Do you want to talk about it?"

"It was awful, babe. It was god-awful." Christine's voice was a shaky, painful murmur.

Andrea caressed her back, but Christine slipped away from her.

"We'll get in trouble," she protested.

Andrea let out a frustrated sigh.

While holding hands for a moment was overlooked by the screws, public displays of affection were strictly forbidden. Anyone persisting in PDA faced the very real possibility of being sent to the Safe Room. To make matters worse, Christine had heard that some girls were being beaten in the Safe Room. The staff, apparently, was taking their cruelty to new extremes.

"Two guards came into our room last night. Just before lights out. And… and… they… " Christine broke into a sob.

Andrea caressed her back and rubbed her shoulder. Christine leaned against her and sobbed.

"God, babe, I… I can see things."

Andrea pulled away and stared into her eyes, holding her firmly by her shoulders. "What do you mean?"

"I can see things before they happen. Or as they happen. I have visions. I've had them since I was a little kid."

Andrea wiped Christine's nose with her right sleeve. "What do you mean you have visions?"

"I saw one of the girls. She was bleeding so badly." She whimpered, then continued, "I think something happened to Julie."

Andrea just stared at her, looking unsure how to respond, or what to say. Maybe she was thinking that her friend, her new lover *was* batshit crazy. Everyone else did, Christine thought.

"She's probably okay, Chrissy. Try to relax."

"I don't think she is!" Christine snapped, then turned and stormed off. "You don't understand!"

Andrea didn't go after her. Christine looked back before heading back inside. Her friend was still there, a motionless shape on the track staring at her, and probably judging her like everyone else had judged her all her life.

Later that day, Christine felt depleted by the visions that blasted through her mind like a fire hose set at high pressure. She didn't want to sit with Andrea at lunch. Something had bothered her and rubbed her the wrong way about her new babe. She couldn't quite place her finger on it, but she didn't really trust her anymore.

Instead, Christine searched for Bex around the caf. She missed her old friend and when she finally spotted her, hanging with Chatterbox and a few others, a guilty feeling plagued her. She ditched her old friend and had focused all of her attention on Andrea since Andrea's arrival at Palisades. Maybe, she figured, she could make amends.

She grabbed her food and sat down across from Bex. She didn't even have to look—she could feel the hard scowl coming from Chatterbox's direction.

"Well, well, well. If it isn't… What's her name again?" Chatterbox said with derision.

"Ladies," Christine greeted, attempting to smile but a feeling of embarrassment began to flit through her.

"So, you're back…" Bex said. "We'll let you sit with us again if you promise us one thing."

Christine felt the heat rise to her face. She had suspected her friends would be annoyed she'd been spending a lot of time with Andrea, but she hadn't realized they'd officially banished her. How was she going to win them over again? "Sure. Tell me. What can I do?"

"To never sit with that cheap slut, Andrea, ever again," Bex said, then slapped Christine's cheek.

The slap surprised her and stung for a few seconds. Christine glanced over toward Andrea, who sat several tables away, mingling with a couple of new girls whose names she didn't care to know. The way her head pointed down made her look sad.

The girls waited for her response. Finally, after a pause, she said, "Yeah, I promise."

"Great," Bex said. "Now we can fill you in on our plan."

"To save Sue?" Christine asked.

"Yup." Bex nodded toward Sarah, and said "We might have a way to get a keycard, which will allow us access to the elevator. Sarah's going to try to get it tonight. And once she has that—"

"Once I have it—" said Sarah, "—we're gonna go down to the sublevel and rescue Sue."

"Holy shit," Christine answered. "It's really happening."

"You bet your ass it is," Bex said, enthusiastically. "You gonna help us?"

"What do you need me to do?"

All eyes gravitated towards the entryway of the caf, and the thrumming chatter dropped to a quiet murmur. Davies had entered. She trotted to the center of the cafeteria. Close behind her trailed Jack, Jill, Carmen, and two security guards. Christine locked eyes with Jack for a moment and he seemed to leer at her.

Davies stopped in the middle of the room and put the microphone to her mouth. "Quiet," she ordered. "There's been a..." she hesitated, thinking about how to frame how she would impart the news to the cohort.

Christine saw glass slicing through flesh. A portent had suddenly flashed in her mind. The sinews looked raw, the blood stained the girl's bra and panties a deep vermilion. She could not see her face, but she knew who the shredded wrists and dark blood belonged to.

"There has been an accident," Davies went on. "One of our girls has passed on."

There was a collective gasp. Christine dropped her head and began to sob. "Please, god. No," she gasped and made quiet whimpery sounds.

"Julie is no longer with us. I know many of you were close with her, and this is very hard for you to process." Davies's eyes panned around the room. They settled on Christine. "I know how difficult it can be to lose someone so close to you. But don't fret, my darlings—" Her voice rose, "We will increase any additional counseling sessions that may be needed in both frequency and intensity. This is something that we've anticipated, and though it is a first for the Palisades Academy, it is something we must deal with and face head on."

"What happened to her?" one of the girls blurted.

Davies looked at the girl who had raised the question.

"What happened was Julie did not follow the protocols of rehabilitation. She did not heed our counselors' instructions. It's a shame, really. The program is tried and tested, but she chose to be difficult—hard-headed. In the end, she just opted to kill herself."

"I'm gonna be sick," Christine said, as she keeled over.

Chatterbox caught her just in time before she fell on the ground. Sarah got up and raced over to help.

"Chrissy," Sarah said, brushing her hair away from her face. "You okay? She stood up and called for help. "We need help over here!"

Suddenly Andrea had rushed over and had interjected in attempting to help Christine.

"We don't need your help!" Chatterbox yelled.

Andrea snapped toward her and yelled, "Bitch, who do you think you are, talkin' to me like that?" In a crouch stance, she cradled Christine from behind.

"We're good, Andrea," Sarah interjected. "Please…"

Davies had made her way over and stood looming over the spectacle. Christine, half out of it and feeling woozy, had heard the bickering and yelling, but she was too out of it to do or say anything.

"What is going on here?" Davies yelled. "Get her off the floor!"

"Chrissy, come on. Get up," Sarah coaxed.

"Jack! Get over here and take her will you?"

In a few seconds, Jack, Carmen, and the guards had a firm hold of Christine and she knew immediately she was in trouble. As she was carried out, she glanced back at her friends and they were looking alarmed. Her head was spinning and her strength had left her and all she could think was, *oh, God, please. Please, not the Safe Room.*

∼

When Christine opened her eyes, she was sitting in a wheelchair and still feeling out of it. She felt groggy, and it reminded her of the times her mother gave her too much Robitussin as a child—leaving her spacey and unable to remember anything. Her stepfather would usually be around and images of his leering face flashed through her mind. She hated this feeling of not having control over her mind.

Inside the elevator, she felt the downward lurch and the corresponding rise in her stomach. The doors opened and the chair was pushed forward into a dark passageway that looked like an underground bunker. There were pipes running along the ceiling, thrumming and clanging noisily, and unpainted cinder block walls lined the passageway.

"Where are you taking me?" she asked.

"Did I say you were allowed to speak?" Davies asked.

Christine was lashed hard across the top of her thighs with a riding crop. She screamed.

"You don't speak unless I say you can," the woman shouted into her ears.

The pain stung and lingered for a while as she continued into the passageway. Then, the chair stopped and was turned. She faced what looked like a dark, old, crumbling jail cell. Her eyes adjusted onto a pale, bony figure laying languidly on a cot. The person (she was unsure whether they were male or female) looked as thin as a rake.

Davies crossed in front and opened the cell door with a large skeleton key. The door groaned open and she was pushed inside. The guards suddenly grabbed Christine from the chair and tossed her onto the dusty floor. Then, Davies and the security exited.

"Jane, I brought you your dinner," Davies said. "It's a very special treat tonight. I think you're going to really enjoy her," she said. "Just a little pork for being such a good girl lately." She laughed. "Did I say pork? I meant perk… just a little perk for acting so proper and well-mannered as of late."

Christine glanced up at the pale figure stirring in the dark and an icy chill spread through her back. A pair of very pale, gangly legs appeared from underneath the tattered blanket and hit the floor. The girl was dressed in an old teddy nightgown that hadn't been washed in ages. If it wasn't a girl, or a living human, then it must be a corpse, she thought—one that had been dug up from the local cemetery and somehow reanimated. Her hair was frayed and there were several bald spots riddled across her scalp. Suddenly, the skeletal thing began making its way over to where Christine lay. As the thing slunk toward her, Christine heard a guttural rasp as if it struggled to breath as it moved.

"Get away from me!"

The girl got up close to Christine's face and opened her mouth. She had sharp teeth on the top and bottom that looked like they'd been filed into points. The way her mouth gaped open—a cavern revealing sharp incisors—reminded her of a grotesque deep-sea fish. A foul odor that smelled of death hit Christine's nose. She stretched out her hand and long, serrated nails scraped her cheek. When she touched her face and examined her fingers, she saw blood.

"Stay away!" She scuttled and kicked her legs in defense of the thing. "Stay the fuck away!"

"You smell nice."

The skeleton had a dainty, female voice, no doubt, Christine thought. *What the fuck happened to her? Jesus.*

The girl lolled her head to one side and Christine thought her neck extended far more than it should've, as if the neck had been severed from the top of the spine.

"Who are you?" Christine asked, crawling backwards. She yelped in surprise when her back hit the bars and she gazed fearfully at the advancing creature.

"I'm Jane."

The girl's sunken, twitching eyes made Christine shudder.

"How long have you been down here for?" She was just

talking now, trying to buy some time. This girl didn't weigh eighty pounds, but that didn't mean Christine wasn't frightened out of her wits. "Listen, no offense or anything, but you are really fucking scary looking."

"No offense taken… I'm not sure," she said, slinking towards Christine. Her legs moved awkwardly as if her knobbly knees had been badly broken and they'd healed without a cast or a proper splint.

Christine, sitting on the ground, kicked her legs out. "Get away!"

"I'm *really* hungry."

"I don't give a shit. Stay the hell away from me!"

Jane lurched toward her and Christine fired a kick that hit her directly in the chest, hurling the skinny mass backwards. She landed on her back and slammed her skull on the ground with a sickening thud.

"Please, I don't want to hurt you," Christine warned, "but if you try to come at me, I'm gonna have to defend myself."

"You're my dinner. I haven't eaten in so, *so long*." Her voice trailed off. She laid still, her arms and legs spread out on the ground.

Christine wondered if she'd hurt her badly. Maybe the girl needed medical attention. "Jane, are you okay?"

She didn't answer her.

"Jane?"

Christine rested her back against the bars and stared at the girl, who remained spread on the ground, immobile like a rock. Several minutes went by and she wondered if she'd killed her.

Then, about half an hour later, Jane slunk off the floor and returned to her cot.

"You're okay?"

"I'm fine," she said. She took a deep breath and wrapped herself in her grimy blanket.

"Can you promise me one thing? That you're not going to hurt me?"

"I can't promise you that," Jane said. Her eyes twitched spasmodically. "You're my dinner, and I'm hungry."

"Fuck…"

Christine's mind raced. She had to come up with a plan and think of one fast. What the fuck was she going to do? She was locked in a goddamn cell with a maniac cannibal that looked like she hadn't been fed in months.

"*Hungry!*" Jane suddenly lurched off the cot and threw herself on top of her.

"Shit, get off me!" She smashed a fist upwards into the thing's nose. Almost instantly, blood gushed out and it sprayed onto Christine, showering her face. Rolling, she got out from under the bag of bones. Something long and sharp flew from Jane's nightie and clinked on the ground. Christine crawled away and used the bars to pull herself back onto her feet. They both saw the metal file lying between them and made a dash for it. Christine angled her shoulder like a battering ram and tackled Jane full steam like a linebacker. She picked up the metal file and pointed it at Jane, who lay sprawled on the ground, clutching her stomach and making awful whimpery sounds. They were reminiscent of a severely wounded animal, Christine thought.

She drifted backwards, keeping her eyes on Jane, until she reached the cell door. A portent flitted through her mind. *Finally, something useful!* Using the file, she jimmied the keyhole until the door creaked open.

"I'm sorry I hurt you," she said as she locked the door behind her. She did feel bad about leaving Jane locked up in the cell, but the damned girl was trying to eat her, for chrissakes!

Christine raced down the forbidding passageway. She had no idea where she was headed but her portent was showing her glimpses of Sue laying down somewhere in a dark cell similar to the one she had just escaped.

She rounded a corner and in another thirty feet, she glimpsed another cell. As she neared it, she saw another pale body shifting in a cot. God, Christine thought, not another cannibal!

The girl stirred and rubbed the sleep from her eyes. She'd been dozing until Christine came along.

She couldn't believe it. "Sue!" she gasped.

Sue yawned and wiped the sleep from her eyes. The faint light emanated from behind Christine, and she realized Sue might not be able to see it was her. "Sue, it's me, Christine." She couldn't believe she'd found her.

"Batgirl?"

"Huh?"

Sue sat upright and the tattered blanket shifted, revealing her pale skin. Bruises mapped her body from head to toe. Christine shuddered at the sight of her. She'd lost a good amount of weight and she was filthy. If Bex were to see her, she thought, she'd go apeshit.

"Are you okay?"

Sue groaned and said, "I'm really hungry. Do you have any food?"

"No, I don't, babe," Christine said, "but I'm gonna get you out of here." She took out the metal file from her pocket and jimmied the cell door. It didn't open as easily as Ghost Girl's had.

"How'd you get here?"

"Long story," Christine replied.

She wiped the sweat from her brow. *Got to get this damned door open. Who knows if and when Davies will be back.*

Finally, she felt something shift in the keyhole and heard a click. The door clunked open and Christine raced inside to grab Sue. "Let's go," she hurried her.

When she placed her hands on Sue, she realized she had to be careful with her. The girl felt fragile, one wrong move or misstep and her ankle might break. "Damnit, what the hell did they do to you?" Christine muttered, guiding Sue out of the cell.

She retraced her steps down the long passageway, heading in the direction from which she'd come. Sue was moving so slowly, and she tried not to panic. *Time is of the essence,* she thought. *Got to get out of this passageway before that vile monster, Davies, comes back and realizes they'd escaped.*

When they reached the corner where the passageway turned off, Christine heard the elevator shaft open and then the clicking of heels. "Fuck," she muttered. She put a finger up to her lips. "We have to go back," she whispered. "It's that bitch, Davies."

The girls turned back and returned to Sue's cell. Christine tried not to panic. What the hell were they going to do? They were going to get caught, and who knows what kind of punishment Davies would conjure for them.

"Maybe you can go back in the cell," Christine said, "and I'll try to hide."

"No," Sue protested, grabbing her arm. She could feel her shaking. "Please, don't put me back in there."

Christine groaned. She felt terrible making her go back inside the cell, but Davies would be on them in a matter of seconds. "We're just gonna have to fight."

"I'll see what I can do," she answered.

Sue was far from a chicken but she was in rough shape, and Christine wondered if she'd even have the wherewithal to walk on her own, or if she'd need to be carried at some point. Christine knew she was going to have to do most of the brawling. Sue's body was too frail. The poor girl. She remembered when she'd gotten to Palisades looking pretty tough and intimidating. She wasn't a big girl per se, but had a personality as big as the Rocky Mountains. Now, she might break something if she were to throw a punch.

They stood there for a moment—Christine trying to decide which way to go, and Sue waiting for direction. But she didn't hear Davies coming. There were no staccato sounds echoing in the distance or the stamping of heels. She should've gotten there by now, she thought. Davies had probably stopped at Ghost Girl's cell! That would be the perfect opportunity to attack her.

"Come on!" She pulled Sue with her and they hurried to find Davies. When they turned the corner they heard the old crone yelling her head off.

"Where is she? *Where the fuck is she?!*"

Christine saw the cell door was opened but didn't see Davies in the passageway, which meant she must've been inside with Jane. Turning to Sue, she told her to "Stay put," then raced toward the cell.

When she got there, sure enough, Davies was in there facing Jane, gripping her riding crop in her right hand, fuming.

"How did she get out?" Davies yelled. "Tell me where she fucking went!" She struck Jane across her face and then whipped her body twice.

Jane screamed and held her arms up defensively.

Christine rushed into the cell and drove the steel file into Davies's back with all her momentum, pushing the woman into Jane. As the file was impaled into her spine, Davies bucked backwards and shrieked, then flopped and fell forward. By the time Christine had removed the file from her back, Jane had already gotten to her. The girl had turned Davies around, had clamped down hard on the woman's face, and had her mounted like a wild jungle animal devouring its prey. Christine saw the key card dangling from Davies's belt, and sprang for it. Once she had a hold of it, she fled from the cell, and made sure to lock it behind her.

On her way back to grab Sue, she heard Davies crying out

obscenities, in agonizing throttles that sounded as though Jane was ripping out her vocal cords.

When she reached Sue, she took her by the arm and guided her back down the passageway. "Come on," she ordered. As they passed Jane's cell, they heard sloppy wet sounds. Christine caught a glimpse of Jane chewing on Davies's flesh and her stomach twisted. Jane, growling with excitement, tugged what looked like the large intestine from her body. For an instant, as they hurried past the cell, Christine thought she smelled the foul odor of the dying woman's insides.

"Don't look," Christine told Sue. "Just keep walking. Hurry."

They reached the elevator. She waved Davies's keycard in front of the sensor, and they heard a rushing noise as it began its descent.

CHAPTER
ELEVEN

INSIDE THE ELEVATOR, Sue pressed her body against Christine. She was depleted. God, the past few nights, Davies had really done a number on her. She tried to forget all the grief that evil wench had caused her, and all the physical trauma she had forced onto her. It was all behind her now, she told herself. That damned bitch got what was coming for her. They say only the good die young. Well, this time the old bag got her due and got it good. And what a way to go. Devoured by a half-starved cannibal.

"Thanks for saving me," Sue said.

"My pleasure," Christine answered.

It felt wonderful to be held so tight. Sue relished her old friend's warmth, latching her shaky fingers around Christine's. If she didn't have her to lean against, she might've collapsed. Her legs were weak and the exhaustion in her bones was indescribable.

"I thought Bex would've been the one to save me."

Christine laughed, then replied, "Wait 'till she sees you. She's been plotting your rescue for weeks now. You have no idea." She shook her head. "That's all she's been talking about. She's gonna be so excited." She shot Sue a grave look.

"We're not out of the woods yet. We're gonna find her, and whoever else wants to break out of this hellhole, and get the fuck—"

The elevator suddenly stopped. Cold air seeped in through the crack in the center-opening doors, then they whooshed open.

About to step onto the elevator was Jack, who shot the girls a perplexed look. Christine let go of Sue and grabbed the steel file from her side pocket. She took a few quick steps toward him and heaved the object into the side of his neck. Eyes wide and unbelieving, his hands clumsily grabbed at the metal file that was lodged deep as blood spurted out like a crimson fountain. Jack gurgled and thrashed. It sounded like he was choking on his own blood.

"That's what you get cocksucker!" Christine yelled, then kicked him in his balls. She went back inside the elevator and placed Sue's arm around her shoulder, and guided her out. They shuffled out of the elevator and went down the long, brightly lit corridor—the one leading past the Safe Rooms—until they arrived at an area of Palisades she recognized.

It must've been very late because no one was in the common area, and luckily they hadn't encountered any of the screws. At least not yet.

"We need to find Bex," Sue whispered.

"That's exactly where I'm going," Christine replied.

The lights were out save for the motion-sensing step lights that turned on as they drifted past.

Once they finally got to Bex's door, Christine peered in through the window. The lights were off but she could see Bex snoozing on the top bunk. Her bare leg was hanging out from the bedsheet. She knocked on the window. "Yo, Bex! Wake up!" They could hear her snoring. "Hey!" she called, careful not to wake up the entire suite. She knocked a few more times until Chatterbox stirred and sat up. *Ugh*, Christine, grumbled. They'd made Bex bunk with Chatterbox. How awful.

Christine swung her arms wildly, signaling it was an emergency. "Open the door."

Chatterbox slunk out of bed and crossed to the door. In a groggy voice, she asked, "What are you doing?"

"We're breaking out of here. Bex!" Christine called out.

Bex had woken up and climbed down from the top bunk and glanced at her, sleepily. "What's going on?" When she saw who was standing behind Christine, her eyes opened wide. "Holy fuck... Sue!" The sight of her old friend had shaken her with mirth. She ran over to her and put her arms around her. "Oh, my god. What did those bastards do to you?"

"We don't have much time," Christine rushed. "Get some things together. Put some clothes on. We need to move. Now—"

"Give me a minute." Bex crossed to her dresser and started flinging clothing and underwear in her backpack.

"We don't have a minute," Christine muttered.

"I'll come with you guys," Chatterbox said. She was already packing a bag. Christine was surprised, not expecting her to want to escape with them.

"Let's hurry up girls."

Once they were all outside the room, Bex asked, "Which way? How are we going to get out? Aren't the doors locked?" Bex looked Christine up and down. "Why are you all bloody?"

"Listen, I wish we had the time to camp out here, sing kumba-fucking-ya, exchange tales about what happened down there—" she wiped sweat and blood from her brow, "—but we have to go. Like now." Christine held up the keycard she'd taken from Davies. "I have the magic key."

"Nice going," Bex said. "Chatterbox, pony up, we're outta here."

As they crept along the shadow-drenched passageways and corners of Palisades, Christine felt like they were a part of a clandestine group, escaping from a heist.

She peered into rooms as they glided toward the exit. The other girls were fast asleep, unaware of their escape. She stopped at Andrea's door and stared in.

She felt Sue tug at her arm.

"I want to get my journal," Sue whispered.

"Seriously?" Christine answered.

Sue nodded. Christine could tell she knew the risk she'd pose but she could see in her eyes how badly the girl wanted it.

Bex turned to her. "I'll get it. I know where it is. I'll be back in a minute." She took off into the dark.

"Your fucking journal?" Christine asked, annoyed. "Really?"

"I wrote down some important stuff about this place," Sue said.

After a few moments, Bex returned with Sue's journal in hand.

"I'll hold onto it for you," she said.

"Come on," Christine ordered.

Nearing the security desk, they arrived at the swinging glass doors. There was no one at the desk. Christine could hardly believe it. The logo for Palisades brought her back to that fateful day when she'd first arrived at the rehab center. Now that she thought about it, she hadn't been through these doors since she first got there. They had only been allowed to enter and exit the building through the backside. The front of the building and the world beyond it had become vestigial, blurring into a clouded, half-remembered reality.

She waved the keycard and the doors *whooshed* open. They quickly crossed the vestibule toward the front door, and with one more wave of the keycard, they were finally free. The air was crisp as they stepped outside. At the bottom of the stairs, they all turned and glanced up at the looming building, taking in the structure one final time and saying their silent goodbyes.

"*Au revoir!*" Bex shouted into the night.

"Since when do you speak French?" Sue asked.

"Since I took it in middle school and high school," she answered, then brought Sue close and kissed her on the mouth. They locked lips for a long time until Christine cleared her throat.

"*Ah-hmm.* Excuse me. This is really sweet and everything, and I wish I could bust out the popcorn, but we should probably keep it moving. You know, so we don't get caught."

The girls released their kiss and they were both grinning like little school girls.

"Yeah, it would suck to make it this far and then get spotted," Sue said.

"Yeah, it would," Christine said.

"Which way should we go?" Chatterbox asked. She'd been quiet until then. Christine almost forgot she had tagged along.

Christine scanned the area and spotted a path that began just at the mouth of a grove of tall trees. It was a hiking path. She recalled one of Palisades's key selling points was advertising all the hiking the girls could do to get out into the outdoors. Other than being allowed brief periods of downtime in the yard, none of them had participated in any of the outdoor activities that had been promised. It was all a complete farce.

She pointed toward the path. "That way."

"Why that way?" Chatterbox asked. "Are you sure there isn't a better way we can go? What if we get lost going through? It's really dark."

"What is this, Twenty Questions?" Christine asked, obviously annoyed that Chatterbox kept interjecting herself in their game plan.

"Yeah, shut up, will you," Bex said.

"We'll take a trail until we get to a road," Christine said. "Once we get there, we can hitchhike and get as far away from here as we can. Someone is bound to stop and help us."

They crossed the manicured lawn and headed for the trail. Christine turned one more time and looked at the building that had been her prison for several months. What would come of it? she wondered. She suddenly wished they had more time and supplies and could somehow burn it to the ground. The problem with torching the place was there were still girls inside, sleeping, resting in the twilight hours.

They got to the dirt path and Christine noticed Sue was slowing down.

"Are you all right, hon?" Bex asked.

Sue grimaced. "My feet."

Bex had given her an old pair of Chuck Taylor's from her room. Admittedly, they weren't the most comfortable shoes for hiking on rocky, dirt paths, but that's all she had.

"Do you need to take a break?" Bex asked.

Sue had stopped and examined her feet. She rotated her ankle. "I think I can keep going."

"Just let us know if you need to stop," Christine said.

Noticing she was falling way behind, Christine yelled back to Chatterbox— "Keep up, will you?" She was annoyed she'd tagged along. It would've been easier getting away without motormouth weighing them down.

Christine held Sue's hand, while Bex carried the bulk of her weight, making sure she didn't trip as they trod along. The winding path was uneven and treacherous; the trees were a dense canopy, blocking all light, making their trail as black as a cave. As they lumbered along, it got darker and darker. They heard the crickets chirping and the cicadas buzzing almost musical, percussive beats.

Chatterbox had been walking like a sloth and Christine was getting upset. She kept glancing back and making sure she was still with them. Caring for Sue and making sure she made it out okay was one thing. Babysitting a fully capable girl was not supposed to be on the agenda tonight. They'd all been through too much and motormouth had to keep up the pace. *Damn her!*

"What are we going to do once we get to a road?" Chatterbox blurted. "I mean look at us. We're half-clothed. Sue looks like she's just been released from a concentration camp. What's the game plan here? We could get in real serious trouble. I mean, why don't we go back?"

"Shut up, will you?" Bex said, not able to hold back her snarky tone. "You said you wanted to come. Now you want to go back? You're really pissing me off, you know that?"

"Shut up? Shut up?" Her voice went up and up. "We might be breaking some kind of law. Let's just go back before something really bad happens."

"The only bad thing that's gonna happen out here," Bex said, "I'm gonna drive my foot so far up your ass, if you don't stop your grumbling, you won't be able to make it out of these woods. Just put a goddamn lid on it."

Chatterbox speed-walked in front of them, darting past them. As she pulled ahead of the girls, she muttered something but Christine couldn't hear what she'd said.

"What was that?" Christine asked.

Chatterbox suddenly bolted away from the pack. They heard the slamming of her feet getting farther and farther away on the path.

"HEY! Where are you going?!" Christine blurted after her.

She didn't stop or respond. The girl kept running deeper into the woods like a startled deer.

"Hold Sue," Christine told Bex. "I'm going after her." Once Bex had a secure hold of Sue, she took off and followed the sound of footfalls pounding the dirt. *Damn! What's this girl's deal?* Chatterbox was getting farther away from them. Christine picked up the pace and ran hard.

In the distance, past several trees and a pile of brush, she saw something bright glowing. Must be Chatterbox, she figured, but what was creating that light?

"Hey!" she called out.

The light moved deeper into the dark. From Christine's vantage, the small light flickered, appearing and then disappearing when it moved behind a tree.

"Stop!"

She didn't feel like chasing Chatterbox but her intuition was gnawing at her, warning that something was amiss.

Chatterbox screamed in the distance. Something had happened to her. *God, what now?* Christine thought. Guided by the fading echoes of the yell, she was careful not to trip over a root or some other obstacle along the path. *Dammit Chatterbox, why are you doing this?* Now, she had to step off the trail and prowl in the dense thicket.

"Christiiiiiiiiine!" It was Bex calling. "Are you *okay??!*"

"Yeah!" she called back.

"Should we come over to you?"

"No, stay put!" Christine yelled. "Once I find her, we'll come back!"

She trudged carefully over a downed tree.

"I hurt my ankle real bad… I don't think I can walk."

"Oh, my fucking god," Christine blurted.

When she got to her, Chatterbox was talking on a cell phone. That's what the light had been! She was sitting on the ground with her knees bent, and her back perched on a massive tree trunk. It looked like she might've tripped and got hurt.

"Who are you talking to?" Christine snapped, then rushed at her. "Where'd you get that fucking phone?"

"Christine is here!" she said. "Please, come get me now!"

"WHO THE FUCK ARE YOU TALKING TO?"

Chatterbox hung up the call and held the phone underneath her. The glow of the phone made her look like an eerie apparition.

"Answer me, will you!" Christine barked. "Who were you talking to?"

Chatterbox flinched and cried out in pain. Her eyes filled with tears. "My ankle—ah, it hurts so bad."

"I don't give a damn!" She got closer. "I want to know—"

It happened so quickly, Christine didn't have any time to react. Chatterbox had taken something out of her sweatshirt pocket and lashed the air with fury. The utility blade made contact and opened Christine's throat, and a spray of red jetted into the night air. Christine put her hands up to her throat and began to gurgle.

Chatterbox sat up, then got to her feet. With a wounded ankle, she shambled toward Chrissy, who turned and tried to step away but she moved very slowly now. Chatterbox caught up to her and stabbed her in the back. Then stabbed her again. And again. Chatterbox slashed her back deeply, and with such force, until Christine collapsed face-forward on the dirt path. Christine was unable to yell out for help, unable to draw any air, as she choked on her own blood. All that escaped her were painful, wet, gurgling sounds.

BEX SUPPORTED the bulk of Sue's weight, thinking if she moved away or left her to stand on her own, Sue would collapse.

"Chuck Taylor's were the best they could do, huh?"

"Sorry about that, hon. Wanna trade with me?"

"What are those, Crocs?"

"Yeah..."

"No, thanks." Sue laughed. "I'll stick with these."

Bex had begun calling out for Christine, yelling her name but receiving no response. Something had happened. A tight, squirmy feeling swirled inside her that told her escaping Palisades wouldn't be so simple.

"Christiiiiiine!" Bex called out. "*Hey!!!* Where are *you?!*"

"Let's go find them," Sue said.

"You sure you can walk?"

"I made it this far. Maybe something happened. We should go look for them."

"Okay. Let's go, but we'll take it slow," Bex said.

Bex held onto her, and they hiked down the path in the direction which they believed they last heard Christine's voice. "Slow and steady. That's it." It was so dark, Bex concentrated on the path and made sure Sue didn't trip or fall. She felt fragile and weak. Bex began to fear something terrible may have happened. What if in her chase, Christine broke her leg, fell and hit her head on a rock. She'd never admit it to Sue, she had to remain poised and strong, so they can get to safety, but she was *very* afraid.

"I hope they're okay," Sue said.

"Me too."

"I just don't understand why she would take off running like that," Bex said. "Now's not the time for a prank like this."

"It's Chatterbox," Sue said. "What do you expect?"

They wandered along the pitch-black trail for another few minutes. Bex called out, "Christ*iiiiine!*"

Still, they received no answer.

"I think I heard something," Sue said. "Over there." She pointed toward the left of the trail.

Bex heard it too. It sounded like leaves rustling. Maybe it was just an animal, like a rabbit or even a deer.

Then she heard the pounding of feet taking off.

"Stop running!" Bex figured it was Chatterbox. "Stay here! I'll be back." She helped sit Sue down on a log, then said, "Don't go anywhere!" and took off after the mystery runner.

As she took flight, she prayed she didn't trip over a root or rock or some other form of debris. One false step and she'd really be done for, then they'd never make it out of there. She wasn't sure if she was a few paces or a few miles from the next trailhead.

In the distance, she saw the glare of a light bouncing through the woods.

"Hey! Chatterbox, stop fucking running!"

She followed the light. Must be a cellphone, Bex figured. How in the world did she get her hands on a cellphone?

The trail opened into a grassy clearing, then a trailhead,

giving way to a two-lane road. The runner definitely *had* been Chatterbox. She could see her clearly now that they were out of the dense trees and were washed in moonlight and speckled stars. Chatterbox seemed injured, darting along with a terrible hobble.

There was a parked van about fifty feet down the road, and it looked like she was heading toward it. A few people congregated outside of it, facing them. Maybe they could help. As she made her way toward them, Bex raised her arms in an attempt to get their attention. "Hey! We need help!"

Chatterbox got to them first and it looked like she was saying something to them. Then she pointed back toward Bex.

"Hey…"

They all got inside the van and went in reverse. Someone suddenly rushed Bex from behind and she felt a syringe plunge into her back.

"*AHHHH!*" she yelped.

Two men grabbed hold of her and led her in the direction of the van.

"*No! Let go of me!*" She thrashed and flailed and tried to get free from their grasps. "You bastards!" When she turned and got a look at them, they were security guards from Palisades. "LET ME GO!" She cried out. "*Fuckers!*"

They held her arms down. She jerked and flailed, but there was no escaping their ironclad grasps, and in a few seconds they were facing the van. The sliding side door heaved open. Bex saw some familiar faces and the realization hit her like an anvil. Raw fear filled her stomach. This might be the end of the road for her. "Please…" she cried. "No… God, no…" Chatterbox was sitting inside, her face was twisted with pain; her hair was mussed. She was complaining about her ankle. They hadn't restrained her. Carmen, one of the head nurses, seemed to be examining her ankle, which had swelled into a massive balloon. The nurse fed her pills, which Chatterbox chased down with water from a plastic bottle.

"Where's Susan?" Jillian, the head counselor, asked.

"She's not with her? She must still be out in the woods," Chatterbox said.

"You traitor!" Bex yelled at her. "How could you?!" She began to sob.

Jillian said, "Oh, quit your whining."

Crammed in the back row was Dr. Hintermeyer, Dwayne, the other nurse, and a fancy-dressed man she recognized, but whose name she didn't know. Their eyes narrowed and they glared at her. The guards shoved her inside and once she was in, the hazy dome light began to dim and so did her consciousness.

Sue stared out her window into the courtyard. The sky was a radiant pink as the sun dipped toward the horizon. There were a few girls outside enjoying the late afternoon air. One small group kicked a soccer ball back and forth. Springtime had finally come and she was glad of it. The long, seemingly endless winter had sent her into a deep, seasonal depression she thought she would never dig herself out of. *This is peace,* she told herself. *This is sanctity.* Just watching the girls playing outside brought her tranquility.

She watched the figures in the distance, strolling around the track. Who were *those* girls? she wondered. One was in a wheelchair and was being pushed by a nurse. The other two looked vaguely familiar, but she just wasn't sure. Everything was so hazy and convoluted lately. Jillian had told her this would be a normal feeling during Phase 3 of her recovery. But she promised her things would get better after several weeks of therapy and more visits to the Safe Room.

Sue braced herself against the desk chair. She felt dizzy. If she hadn't held onto something firm, she was sure she'd have fallen. It had happened a few times already. She'd been hit with random spells of vertigo and would black out only to awaken in the medical room, marked with black and blues and scrapes and other odd wounds.

A flash of an old memory seemed to flitter into her mind. It was dark and there was a very skinny girl talking to her. Whispering. Inside a dark cell. Some kind of dungeon—like something out of a horror movie. God, she tried hard to shrug it off. The psychologist had explained to her that since she'd experienced an inordinate amount of trauma as a young girl and throughout her life, she now suffers from a disorder known as paramnesia, or false, illusory memories. All of the therapy she was undergoing, and all the work she was doing to get better she was told, would help with her disorder. Sue tried hard to stick to and follow her regiment. She knew it was only for her own betterment—to assist her with coping.

Jillian appeared at the door, smiling softly. Sue liked Jillian. She was so caring and easy to talk to. Who knew where she'd be or what she'd do without her support.

"Hi, Susan," Jillian said. "How are you feeling today?"

"I'm doing a lot better." She didn't dare tell her about her horrific, intrusive memory. Perhaps if she pushed it to the back of her mind, she'd forget all about it. "It looks so nice out." Sue lowered her eyes. "Maybe, you think it's possible Jillian, I can go outside soon? One of these days?"

"I think that might be arranged," Jillian answered. "You seem to be making steady progress. I don't think that's out of the question." Jillian smiled at her.

She had such a warm, affectionate smile.

"Dr. Hintermeyer is ready to see you. Are you ready for your session?"

"Yes," Sue said. "I'm ready."

Jillian offered her arm out and Sue latched on, and they walked out of her room, making their way, arm-in-arm. The horrible memories—the false memories that had plagued Sue moments earlier began to dissipate. As she and Jillian walked down the passageway that led to the Safe Room, Sue had already thrust those dreaded memories out of her mind. Even before arriving at the room, she was safe, cocooned in an invisible, primal love.

ACKNOWLEDGMENTS

I am deeply grateful to my family and friends, who remain incredibly supportive of all my writing endeavors. To my cousin, thank you for being the one who reads every word I put on the page. A special thanks to my cover artist, Sanskarans, for consistently bringing my vision to life and offering such steadfast support. Finally, to my editor, Somer Canon—thank you for your sharp eye and for helping me tighten my prose into something I'm proud of.

ALSO BY DAVID LOPERA

The Basement Dwellers

The Netting

9 798995 310112